I0646357

TED TAYLER

A GENUINE MISTAKE

BOOKS

By Ted Tayler

The Freeman Files

Red Herring Season

Gathering Clouds

Still Standing

Vinci Books

vinci-books.com

Published by Vinci Books Ltd in 2025

1

Copyright © Ted Tayler 2021

Chapter One

Monday, 13 August 2018

WHEN GUS FREEMAN arrived in the Old Police Station's car park, he soon realised that the team was back to its full complement. Luke and Neil had returned from their trip to the Yorkshire city of Bradford and parts of that vast county's rugged countryside.

There were just two empty spaces. So Gus drove into one near the middle of the row Geoff Mercer had secured from the County Council. Gus knew Blessing Umeh would arrive in the next few minutes, and his young Detective Constable would appreciate the last space on the right-hand end.

It was small compensation for a wounded heart, but Blessing was a tough cookie. She would get over the loss of PC Dave Smith's affections in time.

Gus travelled alone in the lift. He found Luke Sherman and Neil Davis hard at work. Alex Hardy and Lydia Logan Barre were still preparing for the start of a new week.

Gus nodded to the couple and walked over to chat with Neil and Luke.

He heard the lift returning to the ground floor. Blessing was on her way.

"A quick catch-up, lads," he said. "Then, I'm off to London Road to collect the next cold case."

Neil and Luke brought Gus up to speed on the events of last week.

DCI Phil Banks called on Tuesday afternoon. His team had searched high and low for Jennifer Forsyth's former boyfriend, Kyle Ellison. They found no utility or council tax bills carrying Ellison's details. There was no evidence Kyle had worked or paid National Insurance and Income Tax in the past twenty-five years. The paper trail ended at the flat he'd rented in Leeds.

DCI Banks decided there was only one logical explanation, so he arranged interviews with the people who had wanted Ellison out of their daughter's life. He needed to narrow the search area. Luke reminded Gus that scrubland near Digley Reservoir was already under investigation last Tuesday afternoon. The Reservoir was seven miles from the village of Marsden, where the Forsyth family lived. It was twenty-five miles from Leeds and the last sighting of Kyle Ellison.

Luke had driven north with Neil later last Wednesday morning and reached Trafalgar House in Bradford at two o'clock. Detective Inspector Clemence took charge of the interviews with the male members of the Forsyth family. Neil and Luke watched from an observation room next door as Jennifer's father, Dave, and brother, Darren, adopted the 'no comment' tactic favoured by people who hoped to hide their guilt.

Neil and Luke learned that Jennifer's mother, Mary, had

been more forthcoming in an interview late Tuesday afternoon. It transpired there was no love lost between Mary and her husband.

"We drove to Digley Reservoir late on Wednesday afternoon, guv," said Luke. "Mary Forsyth overheard her husband describe an odd-shaped broom tree near where they dumped Ellison's body after Darren killed him. The remains were in the mortuary on Tuesday evening, but Clemence had kept a forensic team gathering evidence."

"It didn't take long to find the poor devil," said Gus.

"An hour, guv," said Neil. "There was plenty to do before they could close the case."

"Darren Forsyth served three months of his six-month sentence for assault," said Luke. "When he came out, Dave Forsyth was adamant that they needed to get Kyle Ellison out of Jennifer's life for good. He persuaded his daughter to contact Ellison and convince him she wanted to go back to him. Jennifer walked to a bus stop late at night and sat on a bench. As they talked, Ellison arrived on foot, and Darren crept from behind the bus shelter and brained Ellison with a tyre lever. Dave Forsyth then drove up, and Jennifer and Darren helped get Ellison's body into the boot. Darren and his father buried the body half a mile from Digley Reservoir."

"Jennifer moved away from Marsden to Chippenham the following week, guv," said Neil. "Darren got himself a flat in Leeds. The stuff Blessing found on social media was Darren's doing. He set up fake accounts to convince the locals Kyle had moved away to find work."

"Jennifer changed her name to Maddy Mills as soon as she reached Chippenham," said Luke. "Maddy told the truth when she said she kept her whereabouts from her family. They did not know where she was living. Mary

Forsyth took no part in the murder. She was happy to give evidence against her husband. Dave had made her life hell for years."

"Mary Forsyth told them everything she knew to save herself from prison," said Neil. "She didn't know Jennifer lured Ellison to his death on her father's orders. However, she realised what must have happened when Jennifer left home, Darren moved out, and Dave and Darren referred to the burial site in a drunken conversation during a family night in a pub."

"Mary Forsyth was an accessory after the fact," said Gus. "A person who knows something that might help secure an arrest for a serious offence must disclose that information."

"Clemence and his detectives, together with the forensic people, worked on the evidence from the burial site on Thursday and Friday morning," said Luke. "The coroner's report showed that the body was that of a male, aged between eighteen and twenty-four. The cause of death was a single blow to the back of the skull."

"The police had searched for DNA, dental records, and any item known to have belonged to Kyle without luck," said Neil. "So, proving the body was Ellison would be impossible without fresh evidence or a confession."

"Darren was the first to crack," said Luke. "The social media accounts he set up in Kyle Ellison's name sunk him. They have their version of the Hub at Trafalgar House, and the computer whiz kids soon unearthed the dummy email accounts, usernames, and passwords Darren had set up on his laptop. He changed passwords regularly, as the experts suggest you should, but he kept a note of every item in a cardboard box. Then, as Blessing discovered, Darren posted bits and pieces to fool people into thinking the accounts were active."

"It worked, too," said Blessing.

"Did he confess to the murder?" asked Gus.

"Not at first," said Neil. "When we arrived at our B&B on Thursday night, Luke and I thought things were slipping away, but on Friday morning, something from the Digley Reservoir site turned up trumps."

"Darren must have got splashed with Kyle's blood when he struck him with the tyre lever," said Luke. "The forensic team found a bandana lying under the remains. There was nothing to prove that the bloodstains on it were Kyle Ellison's, but they found traces of a second person's DNA."

"Darren Forsyth's?" asked Gus. "Did he wipe the blood from his clothes and face?"

"Yes, guv," said Luke.

"As soon as he saw the evidence bag with the bandana inside, Darren sang like a canary, guv," said Neil.

"Blaming everything on his father, no doubt," said Gus.

"He made me do it. His very words, guv," said Luke.

"What a mess, guv," said Blessing.

"A tragic mess, Blessing," said Gus. "Suzie accompanied Geoff Mercer to Redwing Avenue in Chippenham last Thursday evening to arrest Madeleine Telfer. Suzie told me the confusion on young Oliver's and Emily's faces as their mother left the house in handcuffs will live with her forever. Chris Telfer did not know what secrets his wife had kept buried for so long. He looked broken."

"Can you ask the ACC for something less gruelling later, guv," said Lydia.

"The Duncan case was a puzzle wrapped in an enigma," said Gus. "Churchill said that about Russia, didn't he?

Perhaps it's no surprise that the man who led us to uncover Alan and Maddy's deepest secrets was Russian."

"When did you two get back from Yorkshire?" asked Alex.

"We stayed until DI Clemence spoke with Dave Forsyth," said Neil. "Jennifer's father's supply of no comments ran out. There was a fair bit of swearing, but he realised the game was up. Clemence informed Forsyth as he left the interview room that his daughter was on her way to Bradford from Chippenham. All three would get charged in due course."

"I got home to Warminster at around eight o'clock," said Luke. "Nicky was livid."

"Squash court booked?" asked Lydia.

"No, souffle ruined," said Luke.

"Ouch," said Lydia. "Not a brilliant start to the weekend."

Gus was itching to leave for London Road.

"Has everyone updated their files?" he asked.

Each team member replied in the affirmative.

Gus flicked through the folder on his desk.

"Right, I'll be back in a couple of hours. Try not to miss me."

With that, Gus was in the lift and heading for the car park.

"Right, Luke," said Lydia, "spill the beans."

"We had a row," said Luke. "Not our first by any stretch of the imagination, but our latest cases have meant me working overtime and at weekends. Nicky works, too but sticks to what he calls normal hours. I had promised we'd have a full uninterrupted weekend for a change. How the Duncan case played out in different parts of the country altered that. I could do nothing, but Nicky thought it was symptomatic of my attitude to our relationship. I asked him to marry me six weeks ago, and we bought rings. We debated whether to honeymoon in the Caribbean or the Maldives. What have we done since?"

"You decorated part of the house when Gus gave you time off for good behaviour," said Alex.

"I don't think Nicky considered that a step towards us tying the knot," said Luke. "We were in a DIY store when I proposed. The refurbishments we planned were the catalyst. I suddenly realised that if we were shopping in B&Q, we were getting like our parents, conforming to type. Therefore, we should get married."

"What came out of this summit meeting?" asked Lydia.

"We decided on the Maldives for the honeymoon," said Luke. "As for the date, it will depend on our family's and friend's availability, but we're aiming for late March or early April next year."

"That's great," said Alex. "Cancel any souffle for this Friday night. I think Gus will want to arrange a night out for the Crime Review Team at the Waggon & Horses. We can add that to our list of things to celebrate."

"It's long overdue," said Neil. "If Gus mentions it later, I might call Rick Chalmers. He always enjoys a party."

"Is he married, Neil?" asked Blessing.

"Not these days," said Neil. "You're seeing someone, aren't you, Blessing?"

"Not now, Neil," said Blessing. "At least I'd have someone to chat to, although I didn't think we were compatible when I met him."

"What happened to Dave, your traffic cop?" asked Alex.

"He said he wasn't ready to settle down," sighed Blessing.

"Oh, Blessing," said Lydia. "Men can be dumb, can't they."

"I wouldn't go out with him, but Rick's a good copper," said Neil. "He was a great help on the Stacey Read case. Rick is used to working undercover. I wouldn't have fancied spending hour after hour watching for cars and faces out at the Honda factory. It was tough enough monitoring Rod Maidment's place, where the suspect was static for ten hours a night. He's good company, and that's what you need right now. Don't waste time brooding."

"Rick likes his beer and fast food," said Luke. "He's still one of the lads, even though he's a couple of years older than me. You deserve better, Blessing. Whatever you do, don't miss out on a night out with us if you haven't got a date. We're a team; we'll look after you."

"Thanks, Luke," said Blessing. "I'll be there. Divya might enjoy a night out if her husband is working at the hospital."

"Good thinking, Blessing," said Alex. "Divya worked with Rick and me in the Hub on the Burnside case."

"The Waggon & Horses won't know what hit it," laughed Neil.

GUS POOTLED THROUGH SEEND, climbed Caen Hill, and followed a steady stream of traffic through Devizes. As he parked the Focus in the visitor's car park, he glanced towards the ACC's office window. Kenneth Truelove was nowhere in sight.

After signing in at Reception, Gus took the stairs to the mezzanine two at a time. Vera Butler had her eyes fixed on her computer screen. He could hear Kassie Trotter's distinctive voice advertising last weekend's baking products in the administration area. His unsolicited burst of energy had been a waste of effort.

"Is Kenneth in his office, Vera?"

Vera nodded.

Gus decided it wise to escape to the relative safety of the ACC's office. There was a chill wind blowing on the mezzanine floor this morning. He tapped on the door and entered.

"Geoff Mercer, what a surprise," he said. "Good morning to you too, sir. I bring glad tidings from the Old Police Station office."

"That's enough frivolity for this morning, Freeman," said Kenneth Truelove. "DS Mercer is available again for our weekly review. Thank goodness we can move forward knowing he's with us for the foreseeable future."

"I was going nowhere," said Geoff. "Glad tidings, you said. Did you pull a rabbit out of the hat again?"

"There was nothing magical, Geoff, just old-fashioned, solid police work," said Gus. "The Duncan case proved baffling. But as with several cases the team handled, the answers were there the first time if the detectives involved asked the right questions."

"Please tell me you haven't exposed weaknesses in the work of another respected officer, Freeman," said Kenneth.

"I don't blame Phil Banks, sir," said Gus. "He did what he thought was right. I wouldn't have done any different. If Mrs Campbell-Drake had told him everything she saw on the night of the murder, my team would never have needed to review the case."

"Phil, is it now, not DCI Banks?" asked Geoff.

"I found him easy to get on with, Geoff. You must have rubbed him up the wrong way."

"Take me through your potted version of the case, Freeman," said Kenneth. "I'll try to find time to study the contents of that folder later. Things are hectic here this week."

"I sensed a disquiet outside, sir," Gus said. "I hope it's not catching."

"So do I, Freeman," said Kenneth.

"Right, sir. Let's get on. A moving target is harder to hit. The Duncan murder case was as good as closed once Alex Hardy and I returned from the Isle of Man. The icing on the cake was the arrest of Yuri Kovalev on Wednesday lunchtime. Lydia Logan Barre was right; Duncan's killer was back in the country."

"I'm not entirely up to speed with this part of the case, Freeman," said Kenneth. "Who arrested this Kovalev chap, and what's happening to him?"

"Something bothered me as we drove south from Liverpool," said Gus. "You know how it is, everything seems to have fallen into place, but you can't allow yourself to believe it's over. It kept me awake on Tuesday night, and when I reached the office in the morning, it hit me. The life of the man we left in a tranquil holiday pub on the Isle of Man was in danger. I called the local police and suggested they keep watch on the place. I mentioned your name, sir. That worked like a charm; you'll be pleased to hear. Once I knew that the bar owner was safe, I could relax."

"The fog is clearing, Freeman," said the ACC. "Slowly."

"Sorry, sir," said Gus. "I struggled from the outset with the background information on Alan Duncan and Maddy Mills. Everything pointed to them being in the wrong jobs based on their education and history, yet they seemed content. Phil Banks could never get a fix on the motive behind the murder. After the initial suggestion of suicide, he switched the hunt to find someone who wanted Alan

Duncan dead. He got nowhere. If Lady Davinia had described Kovalev to the officer who received the emergency call, the killer would have been behind bars in no time."

"What first put you on the track of this Russian chap's involvement?" asked Kenneth.

"Oh, that came late in the day, sir," said Gus. "We spent ages talking with people in Biddestone, Corsham, and Chippenham before Blessing Umeh stumbled on a photo of Alan Duncan taken in Moscow. The victim's mother had several photos in a drawer, including one of Yuri Kovalev, but Phil Banks never got to see them. It's not common to search the home of a murder victim's parents, where the said victim lived five miles away with a partner."

"I assume uniformed officers visited the parents to notify them of their son's death, confirmed they had an alibi, then left them to grieve?"

"Exactly, sir," said Gus. "At that point, it could still have been suicide. The next day, they had no reason to return to Corsham when the coroner reported strangulation as the cause of death."

"It was heartening to hear that the Hub helped to solve the case," said the ACC.

"We couldn't have done it without their help, sir," said Gus. "The answer lay in the photographs that Alan Duncan sent his parents. We had seen those early in the piece but didn't appreciate their significance. Maddy Mills was hiding a secret, and my attempts to uncover it delayed the deeper analysis of those photographs. The pictures from Moscow sped up the process because, at last, I could see a plausible reason for Duncan's murder. I suspected a submariner or a colleague not in those photos. Somebody that the men had in common."

"You got little right until the very end, did you, Gus?" said Geoff Mercer.

"Possibly not," said Gus, "but it wouldn't be the first time that a lightbulb moment saved the day in a case you handled, would it?"

"Fair comment," said Geoff.

"I can think of several," admitted the ACC.

"Duncan and Lambert enjoyed a bet on the horses," said Gus. "Nothing wrong with that in moderation, but they let things get out of hand. Rather than ask their colleagues to get them out of trouble, they hatched a plan to pretend to sell secrets to the Russians. I thought Duncan working as a draughtsman in a small company was odd, but although people mentioned he was a stickler for getting things right, nobody said he was a master at his craft. I can't imagine how tough it must have been to produce something that fooled Russian engineers for two decades. Ultimately, they realised their mistake and sent Kovalev to find Duncan and kill him."

"Lambert was Duncan's partner-in-crime, I take it?" said Geoff Mercer, "and the bar owner you referred to earlier."

"He was the group's so-called racing expert," said Gus. "Bob Duncan noticed a missing photograph taken at the Happy Valley racecourse in Hong Kong. Lambert appeared in just one of the group pictures. More often than not, he was behind the camera. I should have kept digging into why it went missing. Duncan took it with him from his parent's home on Sunday before he died. It was a desperate ploy. Kovalev wasn't interested in the cash that Duncan withdrew from the bank, nor in a photograph of Lambert. His mission was to kill Duncan."

"If Mrs Campbell-Drake had told the police everything,

you would never have discovered this Lambert character," said the ACC.

"True," said Gus, "nor would we have learned that Lambert tried to hide his connection to Duncan and the misleading drawings by assuming the identity of his dead colleague, Freddie Watts. That's another spin-off offence that resulted from this case. Add that to the eventual exposure of the secret that Maddy Mills, or Jennifer Forsyth, had buried for twenty-odd years; then it has to be one of the most complex and distressing cases I've handled."

"Distressing?" asked the ACC. "In what way?"

"I went to Chippenham with DI Ferris the other evening, sir," said Geoff Mercer. "We arrested Madeleine Telfer in her kitchen and then had to escort her through the hallway in front of her husband and two children. All three were innocents in this case."

"A tangled web, gentlemen," said the ACC. "What are the odds that Kovalev will stand trial here?"

"Slim," said Gus. "I haven't spoken with our colleagues in Douglas today. They still had Yuri Kovalev under lock and key on Friday. The Russians have no embassy on the island, and as a Crown Dependency, the Manx government can set some of its laws. They defer to the UK Government to handle their foreign affairs. So, as long as Kovalev remains on the island, it could be ages before the Russians can apply diplomatic pressure to release him."

"I remember a Polish criminal hiding on the island last year," said Geoff. "He had found out that European arrest warrants weren't valid there. With these smaller dependencies, the paperwork here on the mainland doesn't always account for every eventuality. The Ministry's pen-pushers often cover the things that might need a proper procedure."

"As my name appears to carry weight in Douglas, I

might suggest they liaise with you, Mercer," said the ACC. "A member of your team should take this case forward now that Freeman has done the groundwork."

"Good idea, sir," said Gus. "When you speak to the locals, Geoff, make sure that the second they hear from the Russians, they must spread the word. *'Russia bullies a tiny island in the Irish Sea.'* The negative publicity could encourage them to cut comrade Kovalev adrift."

"Leave it with me," said Geoff.

"Is there another cold case in your in-tray waiting to pounce, sir?" asked Gus. "My team wondered whether there was any chance of the next one being a piece of cake."

"I have a stack of case reviews on my desk, Freeman," said the ACC. "I grab the first one off the top every time. Your team will have to get used to taking pot luck."

Kenneth Truelove lifted the weighty file from the pile and perused it.

"This case is more recent," he said. "Only six years ago. Someone shot the poor devil on his doorstep on the outskirts of Trowbridge. Gerald Hogan was a fifty-four-year-old financial services professional who worked as a financial advisor, providing investment management and evaluating tax strategies for a range of clients. Gerry, as his friends and family called him, was playing snooker with his two sons, Sean and Byron, at their home on Trowle Common. Sean was eighteen and Byron sixteen. Gerry's partner, Rachel Cummins, a thirty-year-old personal trainer, was in the home gym."

"That could make for an interesting family dynamic," said Gus.

"Get your mind out of the gutter, Freeman," said the ACC.

"Sorry, sir. I'm sure whoever handled this case first asked the right questions. The murder file will highlight any shenanigans."

"The financial services game must pay well if Hogan had a large enough property to accommodate a snooker room," said Geoff Mercer.

"If I might finish the outline of the case, gentlemen," said Kenneth. "The attack occurred on Sunday, the sixth of May, at half-past six in the evening. Gerry and the boys were having a few frames before watching the World Championship final from The Crucible Theatre in Sheffield. The doorbell rang once, but nobody reacted in the games room. The boys hadn't heard it because they had the TV on for the build-up to the evening session. Rachel had to towel herself down and dash from the gym to the front door. On the doorstep, she found a man, half-turned away from her, who asked for Gerry Hogan. Rachel was annoyed at getting dragged away from her fitness routines. She left the man outside while she dashed towards the games room at the back of the house and shouted for her partner."

"Could she supply an accurate description of this man?" asked Gus.

"Rachel carried her towel to the front door," said the ACC. "She told the detectives she was more interested in covering her sweat-covered top half and not giving this guy or the neighbours a cheap thrill."

"The gunman didn't register then," said Gus.

"Ms Cummins said he was tall, white, and casually dressed. As she didn't get a look at his face, she couldn't give the police an accurate assessment of his age. As she said to DI Kirkpatrick in 2012, it was unusual for someone to turn up uninvited, but she never queried why this man wanted to speak to Gerry."

"What happened next?" asked Gus.

"Rachel returned to the gym. The sons told the police they carried on the game they were playing. All three were too far from the front door to hear anything that happened on the doorstep."

"What about the neighbours?" asked Gus. "Did nobody hear raised voices, sounds of a scuffle or an argument? The attack occurred early on a Sunday evening. You can guarantee there would be a dog walker somewhere in the vicinity. Couldn't the police find someone on their way to or from a church?"

"We know it was a sizeable property, Gus," said Geoff. "The name of the area where they lived suggests wide and open spaces surrounding it. So my first question would be, how did the killer get there? Was he on foot? Did Rachel Cummins see a car outside on the roadway?"

"A neighbour heard a motorcycle accelerating past his house that evening," said Kenneth. "He couldn't be sure of the time, but he heard it backfire, and then it buzzed past, sounding like an angry wasp. Ms Cummins said there was no car in their driveway. She was only at the door for a few seconds. The last thing she wanted to do was stand in a sports bra and lycra bottoms talking to a stranger."

"I doubt the motorcycle connected to the murder as it wasn't a high-powered machine," said Gus. "Perhaps the sort of moped a teenager might ride? What about the backfire the neighbour mentioned?"

"Let me run through the sequence of events we can verify," said the ACC. "The front doorbell rang at around six-thirty. Rachel Cummins answered the door, and only ten seconds later, she was hurrying to the back of the house to call her partner. Gerry left the games room to talk to the man on the doorstep. Rachel returned to the gym. Sean and Byron finished the frame of snooker they were playing when their father left. Sean opened the games room door at six-forty-five. The front door was half-open. Sean called out to his Dad that Ronnie O'Sullivan and Ali Carter would soon get introduced to the crowd. The boys were keen not to miss a ball getting potted. Rachel heard Sean shout and decided the interruptions to her exercising had destroyed the mood. She donned a t-shirt and went to the hallway to see what kept her partner. Rachel peered around the door to find Gerry lying on the gravel outside. He'd been shot in the head at close range. A single shot to the temple."

"Well, that changes everything," said Gus.

"Why?" asked Geoff Mercer. "The neighbour said he heard a backfire, and then a motorcycle went past his house."

"The man Rachel saw might not be our gunman," said Gus. "Would Gerry Hogan step outside to talk to a stranger who might have posed a threat? It's more likely he would stand inside his home with one hand on the door for security. He would want to get rid of the bloke quickly. Remember what Gerry and his sons had planned for the evening. If Gerry knew the man well, he might have invited him indoors. Then there's the conversation itself. Gerry was a financial professional. Did this casually dressed stranger want advice on which ISA to use or which stocks and shares were worth a look? Was everything Gerry Hogan dabbled in strictly legal? Few professionals conduct business on a Sunday evening. Did Gerry step outside, away from the house, to chat with the man? Maybe he didn't want Rachel to hear what they said."

"You're right, of course, Freeman," said the ACC. "The time lag between the doorbell ringing and the discovery of the body left things open for conjecture. DI Kirkpatrick treated the entire episode as an extended argument between Hogan and the killer. That may have been remiss of him."

"Kirkpatrick could have got it right," said Gus. "We'll need to explore both avenues. The two men could have had a brief conversation, and then the man left. Sean didn't shout for his father to remind him of the time until six forty-five. There was plenty of time for someone else to approach the property in the twelve or thirteen minutes between Gerry arriving at the open door and discovering his body. We can't know how long that gap was without finding the man who rang the bell at six-thirty."

"If there was another man," said the ACC.

"Nothing is ever straightforward, is it," said Geoff.

"I'll take the folder back to the office," said Gus. "Somewhere in the volumes of material that they gathered, there has to be a clue as to motive. Who wanted Gerry Hogan dead, and why?

Chapter Two

GUS DROVE LEFT the London Road car park without further ado. There was no chance of a brief conversation with Vera and Kassie today. Grace Packenham stood on the far side of the room outside Rhys Evans's office, keeping watch.

When he drew up behind the Old Police Station, Gus took another look at the passenger seat's weighty folder.

"Who was Gerry Hogan?" he asked.

Gerry Hogan was born in the Royal United Hospital, Bath, on March the fifth, 1958. His parents were Peter and Jean Hogan, whose daughter, Belinda, had arrived three years earlier. The family lived in Bradford-on-Avon, a small town of around nine thousand people located six miles from the Roman city of Bath. Gerry attended Christchurch Primary and later Fitzmaurice Grammar School. His headteacher at Fitzmaurice remembered him as well-mannered, good-natured, and intelligent.

Nick Barratt, a close friend throughout their schooling, remembered Gerry as a focused individual. Gerry had his goals mapped out from an early age. No way was he the sort of lad who'd get caught underage drinking, shoplifting, or getting involved with the wrong crowd. Gerry did his utmost to steer clear of trouble. After school, he went to Bristol University to study for a Business and Finance degree. He graduated in 1980 and, after a gap year in Australia, joined the newly formed Hargreaves Lansdown company.

While on his travels, Gerry met his first wife, Evelyn, a wildlife photographer. It was a whirlwind romance. The pair got engaged only weeks after meeting on Bondi Beach. When Gerry returned home to Bradford-on-Avon to start work, Evelyn stayed in New South Wales to complete an assignment at the Macquarie Pass National Park. One month later, she flew into Heathrow Airport and lived with Gerry and his family in Bradford-on-Avon until their registry office wedding in early 1982.

Evelyn continued her career in the UK, accepting commissions closer to home. She made regular trips to West Wales, Richmond Park in London, the Cairngorms in Scotland, and the Farne Islands off the Northumberland coast. The couple bought a place in Clifton, Bristol, that suited them, both for its proximity to Gerry's job and transport links for Evelyn but also for the nightlife they enjoyed as a young professional couple.

A decade later, Gerry wanted to branch out independently and find a family home closer to his parents. They had fallen in love with the Trowle Common property at first sight. It altered somewhat in the next ten years as Gerry's business prospered and Evelyn stopped travelling long enough to give birth to Sean and Byron. They extended the property to one side and at the rear. The sunroom was Evelyn's choice on the ground floor. The games room to the side of it was Gerry's pick for somewhere he could spend what free time he had with his boys.

Evelyn had transformed the spare bedroom into her studio. She explained to Gerry that the direction of the window made a huge difference in light quality. North-facing windows always have soft light because the sun never directly shines through them, while South-facing windows should expect direct sunlight for a good portion of the day. Gerry knew why his wife couldn't resist that dig. Evelyn missed the Australian sunshine.

Sean and Byron were aged eight and six and attending Fitzmaurice Primary in Bradford-on-Avon when Evelyn decided she'd exhausted the most lucrative assignments the UK could offer. The wanderlust was tough to get out of her system. Gerry's business went from strength to strength, so he let Evelyn fly back to Australia for a month with his full support. She returned to the Macquarie Pass National Park to follow up on the work she'd carried out in 1981.

Macquarie Pass is a five-mile-long section of the Illawarra Highway passing through the National Park. The pass links the town of Robertson to the coastal town of Albion Park, where Evelyn rented an apartment.

The pass descends via a narrow roadway with several single-lane sections. It's mostly two lanes with double lines showing no overtaking. This roadway section is very steep and contains many hairpin bends, resulting in buses and trucks needing to back up on some curves. The pass was notorious for accidents, requiring drivers and motorcycle riders to be cautious. After heavy rain, the Macquarie Pass could be closed because of flooding on its top half.

In early March 2002, Evelyn returned from a day photographing egrets, ibis, and herons. A motorcyclist came around a hairpin bend on the wrong side of the road, and she swerved to avoid it. Evelyn's rental car rolled over, somersaulted the safety barrier, and she was dead before the emergency services could arrive from Albion Park. Evelyn was just forty years old.

Gerry Hogan flew to Sydney and met Evelyn's parents for the first time since he and his wife got engaged. The couple couldn't afford to visit the UK for the wedding. Evelyn kept in touch by phone and letter in the intervening years, and Gerry kept promising they would fly out one day so that Sean and Byron could meet their grandparents.

Gerry knew that his in-laws didn't want their daughter to lie in a grave in England. He agreed they should scatter Evelyn's ashes in the Macquarie Pass National Park. When he flew home towards the end of March, he faced up to life looking after Sean and Byron alone.

His sister, Belinda, was always ready to offer a helping hand. When the police talked to her after Gerry's death, Belinda said he had been a brilliant father. He never complained about the cards life had dealt him. Instead, he wholeheartedly threw himself into being the best father to those two boys.

Gerry met Rachel Cummins five years later, in 2007. Belinda worried it was too soon. She was concerned that the boys would find it difficult to adjust. Sean was thirteen, and Byron was eleven by that time. They both attended St Laurence School in Bradford-on-Avon. Gerry and Rachel dated for several months before Gerry introduced her to the boys. They went on holiday to Portugal in the Algarve in the Spring of 2008. Rachel moved into the house on Trowle Common when they returned home.

Gus flicked through the folder to find anything on Rachel Cummins. Who was she? What first attracted her to the wealthy and successful business owner Gerry Hogan?

That might be simple enough to fathom, but although Gerry Hogan was old enough to be her father, two teenage boys were in the mix to consider. Rachel might not be a gold-digger after all. Gus knew all too well that two people from different generations could fall in love.

The Rachel Cummins file was far slimmer, not unlike the lady herself, based on the photograph at the top of the first page.

Rachel was born in the first week of January 1982 in Haslemere, Surrey. Her parents were Jeffrey and Katherine Cummins, who lived and worked in the small town twelve miles from Guildford. Rachel's parents separated eighteen months after Rachel was born, and Katherine raised Rachel alone.

After leaving Woolmer Hill Technology College, Rachel continued her studies to gather a bundle of health, exercise, and fitness diplomas. Then, aged twenty, she started a business as a personal trainer. Rachel continued to live with her mother in Haslemere, driving to various sites across the county for group fitness sessions. She also secured one-to-one appointments with clients in their own homes to boost her earnings.

In 2005, Katherine Cummins reconnected with an old school friend through Facebook, and Rachel arrived home from a fitness session to learn that her mother was eager for Lawrence Wallace to move in.

Rachel thought Lawrence was a creep, but it was her mother's life. Perhaps it was time to plough her own furrow? Three months after Lawrence moved in and several rows with her mother, Rachel moved out. She did her best to find other trainers to accommodate her regulars, and after she was satisfied with her efforts, she moved to Bath. Rachel didn't know the city except by reputation, but her training and experience were transferable anywhere in the country.

After a rocky few weeks where she wondered whether she had made the right decision, Rachel's business soon grew. Eighteen months after moving to Bath, Rachel ran one of her regular fitness classes in Bradford-on-Avon when Gerry Hogan arrived.

Gerry was forty-nine, a widower, and although he ran a successful business, he knew that two decades without regular exercise was playing havoc with his waistline. After the first occasion that he attended her class, they spoke briefly about what he wanted from the sessions. Gerry had told her he'd concentrated on caring for his two sons after losing his wife in a car accident. He needed to get fit for their sakes, and the hour at the gym with her would be the only social interaction he'd get without the boys tagging along.

Rachel had found herself thinking of Gerry during the following week and looked forward to seeing him again. She asked if he wanted to go for a drink after the following Thursday evening session. That was something she had never done before with any of her clients.

Rachel had had to fend off the odd amorous bloke who thought an appointment in his home promised something that was not on the published price list, but Gerry was different. She felt an instant attraction, and later that night, after the drink in the pub, Rachel discovered Gerry felt the same way.

It was the first time he'd been with a woman since his wife died. Despite Belinda's reservations, Gerry and Rachel grew closer, and after that foreign holiday in 2008, Rachel moved in, and for four years, everything was fine.

After Gerry's murder, some issues need sorting out.

Gerry and Rachel had never married. Belinda received the money in the will, but the home on Trowle Common and the financial services business passed to Rachel. Gerry had altered his will after Evelyn's death so that if anything happened to him before the boys reached the age of majority, his sister, Belinda, would act as their guardian.

Gerry altered his will again in 2011. He and Rachel had lived together for three years by then, and there were no clouds on the horizon as far as he could see to stop them from staying together for many years. Sean was already almost seventeen, and the need for a guardian seemed superfluous. Although Byron was two years Sean's junior, what could go wrong?

"Eighteen is the age when minors cease to be considered such," he'd told Rachel. "They can assume control over their actions and decisions at that stage. I'm hoping we can see them married and with their own children before we worry over the provisions of my will again."

From the sixth of May 2012, that worry transferred to Rachel Cummins when her partner got killed. It soon became apparent that Belinda Hogan wished to challenge the will. She told friends she believed Rachel hired a hitman to kill Gerry. Belinda thought that was her plan all along; to live with him for a short period and then cash in.

Gus closed the file for now. This case had more angles than he'd imagined when the ACC walked through it earlier. He vaguely remembered a bloke in a suit coming to their home in Downton one evening to help him and Tess fill out a form. In the event of, and so on, but like Gerry Hogan, they'd thought nothing untoward would happen to them.

They expected to grow old gracefully, and the surviving spouse would inherit the lot when one of them died. That meant they carried on pretty much as before, like millions of other couples whose wills were simple and straight-forward.

After Tess died and the usual rush of urgent official paperwork, Gus couldn't recall what he'd done with their will. He certainly hadn't thought it necessary to amend it. He was only fifty-eight. What was the rush?

As Gus sat in the Focus, staring at the back wall of the Old Police Station, he realised that he'd better find that brown envelope and start thinking about how the wording needed to change. Suzie might not be in a rush to become the second Mrs Freeman, but there was someone else to consider.

GUS GRABBED the folder and travelled up in the lift.

"Welcome back, guv," said Lydia. "My word, that's a big one."

"Don't even think about saying anything, Neil," said Gus.

"Me, guv?" said Neil. "I'm pure in thought and mind. That was what the actress is supposed to have said to the bishop, too."

"We have the murder file here for a financial advisor, Gerald or Gerry Hogan," said Gus. "Hogan died on his doorstep at the beginning of May 2012."

"That we're looking at it now implies the original investigation got nowhere, I assume?" said Blessing Umeh.

"You've got it in one, Blessing," said Gus. "Right, the usual procedure, please. Get the crime scene photos up on the walls and whiteboards. We need photos of the key players and their backgrounds—a Trowbridge and Bradford-on-Avon map that allows us to focus on the murder site on Trowle Common. Luke, you can set up meetings with witnesses and the surviving family members. Alex, I want you to put Gerry Hogan's business life under the microscope. I'll run through the sequence of events in a moment, but if someone wanted Hogan dead badly enough to shoot him in the head in broad daylight, money probably figures in the affair somewhere."

Gus opened the large folder on Blessing's desk, and Lydia joined her colleague to sort through the items they needed.

"I was right. This file carries a lot more detail than we're used to," she said.

"At least someone had the decency to prepare an index," said Blessing. "We'll find the major items so much easier."

Gus returned to his desk and rang Geoff Mercer at London Road.

"Geoff, what happened to John Kirkpatrick?"

"He transferred to Portishead," said Geoff. "John Kirkpatrick's a Detective Chief Inspector with Avon & Somerset."

"I can see a pattern developing here," said Gus. "Every officer I need to contact has got promoted since handling a murder case that the ACC gives me. Is that the reward for failure these days?"

"Cheeky," said Geoff. "They could have had a decent clear-up rate for all you know. Not as stellar as yours, of course, Gus. You get to tackle the occasional blip in their careers."

"If you say so, Geoff," said Gus. "I suppose Victoria Bennison has moved on from being a Detective Sergeant?"

"Vicky Bennison left the police, Gus," said Geoff. "I can get her contact details to you if you need to speak to her, but I can't guarantee she'll cooperate. Vicky transferred to Thames Valley to work in Oxford a couple of years after the Hogan case. In June 2015, she joined officers policing an anti-austerity protest march on a Saturday afternoon in central London."

"One of those marches that started with good intentions but got infiltrated by anarchists, I imagine," said Gus.

"There were many undesirable elements that attached themselves to the peaceful protestors, and things turned nasty," said Geoff. "A male colleague went into the crowd to make an arrest. Vicky saw him quickly surrounded by four or five heavies and waded in to help. Someone behind her shoved Vicky hard in the back, and she hit the ground. While other officers struggled to control the situation ahead of where she fell, Vicky took a severe kicking from the thugs who remained. Every time she opened her eyes to identify her attackers, she saw a sea of mobile phones filming the attack. A dozen officers ended up in the hospital that afternoon. Her male colleague didn't return to duty for fifteen months."

"What about Vicky?" asked Gus.

"Like many other officers, she joined the police to protect the public," said Geoff. "When Vicky shouted for their help, all they did was laugh and keep filming. After the Chief Constable handed her a medal, she threw it in the nearest waste bin and walked away."

"Send me her details, Geoff," said Gus. "I'll tread with care if I ask for her opinions on the case. Thanks for the heads up."

Gus looked around the room. He hoped that none of the Crime Review Team ever suffered like Vicky Bennison. Whatever happened to respect for authority? If only they could rewind the clock to the days when he joined as a uniformed constable. Things were far from perfect in the mid-Seventies, but his old Sergeant would have kittens if he saw what the world was like today. Ah, well, time to move on. At least the walls and whiteboards carried everything they needed for the next few days.

"Right," he said. "A quick summary, and then I want your first impressions. Gerry Hogan lived in Bradford-on-Avon as a child. After university, he joined a well-known financial services firm in Bristol. Hogan married an Australian girl, Evelyn, in 1982 and set up his own business in 1992. They had two sons, Sean and Byron, born in 1994 and 1996. In 2002, Evelyn died in a traffic accident in Australia. She was a wildlife photographer who had worked in the UK throughout their marriage. Before leaving New South Wales, her last commission to live in the UK had been at the same location. The trip back home was to take photographs she could use to compare the wildlife volumes in the Macquarie Pass National Park after a twenty-year gap. The climate change fraternity was eager to see the results. Gerry Hogan didn't cut back on his business involvement but spent every spare minute of free time looking after his sons. His older sister, Belinda, did her best to support her brother. In 2007, Gerry Hogan met Rachel Cummins, a personal trainer. There was a significant age gap, but the couple stayed together, and the boys liked her. Everything seemed fine in the relationship. There were no problems with the business. Rachel Cummins continued to operate her business, holding fitness and exercise classes in and around Trowbridge and Bradford-on-Avon."

"I think I've seen her adverts in the local press," said Neil.

"You never thought of signing up?" asked Lydia.

"Can you picture me in lycra?" asked Neil.

"That's an image I'll never get out of my head now. Thanks a bunch," said Luke.

"Any sensible comments before I move on?" asked Gus.

"Sorry, guv," said Neil.

"On Sunday the sixth of May, six years ago, Gerry and the boys were in the games room at the right-hand rear of the house. Rachel was exercising in the gym on the left-hand side, on the ground floor and at the back. The door-bell rang at six-thirty in the evening, and Gerry and the boys stayed put, meaning Rachel had to stop what she was doing to answer the door. A man stood in the driveway, not facing her head-on but half-turned away. Rachel was in a rush. She opened the door, and the man asked for her partner by name, nothing more. Rachel pushed the door to and made for the games room. She shouted for Gerry and told him someone wanted to speak to him. Rachel returned to the gym. Gerry went to the doorstep to talk to the visitor. At a quarter to seven, Sean left the games room to look for his father. He called out, thinking he was outside in the driveway as the front door was still ajar. Rachel heard Sean call out and stopped exercising. She walked into the hallway, peered around the front door, and found Gerry dead on the gravel. Someone had shot him in the head."

"No known enemies," said Neil.

"A happy relationship," said Blessing.

"Hogan wasn't known to the police," said Luke.

"Déjà vu," said Alex, "all over again."

"It sounds like we've been here before, doesn't it?" said Gus. "We start our review with more information available than with some cases we've handled. The detective who was Senior Investigating Officer on the case now works at Portishead. DS Mercer has told me that DCI John Kirk-patrick will be available to clarify any of the methodologies they followed. His second-in-command, DS Bennison, has left the service. I'll track her down if we need her input and have a quiet chat."

"Vicky Bennison, guv?" said Neil Davis. "We joined around the same time. I remember when she got injured in London. Her head was never right after that. The physical wounds healed within a month, but the mental scars never left her."

"If you knew Vicky when you were both raw recruits, Neil, it makes sense for you to come along. A friendly face might persuade her to give us a helping hand."

"What lines of enquiry did the investigation follow, guv?" asked Alex Hardy.

"After interviews with family and neighbours on Monday and Tuesday following the murder, they were struggling," said Gus. "Nobody saw the man who rang the doorbell arrive or leave the house. Rachel couldn't give the police anything other than a vague description."

"That should have made the SIO suspicious, guv," said Lydia. "Once the sister started spreading the rumour that Rachel had hired a hitman."

"Belinda didn't raise her concerns with her friends until she learned of the provisions in her brother's will," said Gus. "After his wife's death, Gerry had written a new will. So if something happened to him, Belinda would become the boys' guardian until they reached eighteen."

"There must have been another will," said Neil. "If the will with Belinda in it was still valid, Rachel had nothing to gain by bumping off her partner."

"A year before his death, Gerry told Rachel he wanted to amend his will so that she inherited most of his estate. Gerry left money in a trust for the boys to receive when they reached twenty-five. He also made financial provisions for his sister, but Belinda would no longer need to look after his boys. All things being equal, they would be grown men with their own families by the time any will came into effect."

"True, Neil," said Alex. "Nobody could foresee the events of May the sixth. The murder file states that Gerry discussed the new will with Rachel in detail. They both agreed it was the right thing to do. At thirty, Rachel hadn't got around to making a will herself, and she admitted to Kirkpatrick and Bennison that although she and Gerry had lived together for four years, they were in no rush to get married. Rachel hoped it would happen in the future, but it wouldn't have damaged their relationship if it didn't. She loved him as much as she had within weeks of their meeting."

"Sean and Byron confirmed that their father's feelings for Rachel hadn't altered in the months before the murder," added Lydia. "Byron told DI Kirkpatrick, 'They were loved-up. We called her Rachel, not Mum. She never tried to take Mum's place, but she made Dad happy, and we all got on together. There were never any arguments.' Sean added that their Dad dealt with them when they had the odd teenage tantrum. Rachel never interfered, but when he was suffering after getting dumped by a girl he'd liked, Rachel had listened to him and offered him advice."

"The family situation appears idyllic," said Blessing. "The sister's claims don't seem to hold water, guv."

"Belinda Hogan might have been jealous of Rachel Cummins," said Neil. "After Gerry lost his wife, his sister was the first person he'd asked to look after the boys. She was single, with no children of her own, and for around five years, she assumed a mother's role. Gerry amended his will to accommodate that situation. She would have gotten the lot if he'd dropped dead of a heart attack in 2007. A year later, Gerry had a new girlfriend. The boys didn't need Auntie Belinda to look after them any longer. Belinda did not know that Gerry had amended his will yet again."

"But you can understand why he did what he did," said Alex. "It seems quite sensible. Gerry set money aside for the boys and stipulated that they shouldn't get their hands on it and squander it in their teens. So they would be better prepared to cope with a sudden financial windfall when they reached twenty-five. Belinda was also going to inherit a sum of money. Based on the sort of bloke that Gerry Hogan appeared to be, that would be a sum that reflected her input to the family after Evelyn's tragic death."

"Two hundred thousand pounds, Alex," said Gus.

"His financial services business *was* doing well," said Luke.

"In the vital first forty-eight to seventy-two hours of a murder case, the detective team did everything one might expect," said Gus. "The only neighbour that hinted at what might have happened lived half a mile away. He heard what he thought was an engine backfiring, followed by a motor-cycle speeding past his house. Now, it's possible the murderer arrived on a motorcycle, argued with Gerry Hogan, shot him, and then escaped on the bike."

"Why only possible, guv?" asked Blessing. "It sounds plausible to me."

"I'm not saying it didn't happen that way, Blessing," said Gus. "When the ACC ran through the report this morning, I found the timing interesting. Rachel answered the door when it rang at six-thirty; she called Gerry, who went to see what the man wanted. Sean didn't leave the games room until six forty-five. The neighbour couldn't confirm the time that he heard the motorcycle. There was too much of a gap between Gerry reaching the front door and Rachel discovering the body a little after six forty-five. It's unlikely, I admit, but someone else could have visited the house after the first man left. The motorcycle needn't be involved in any way, shape, or form. The neighbour's recollection of a sound he heard on Sunday evening could have been anywhere between six o'clock and nine."

"When did Belinda learn about the new will?" asked Lydia.

"She contacted the family solicitors on Tuesday morning," Gus said. "In the will that Belinda believed was relevant, she was the sole executor. Belinda soon learned that another will existed where Rachel Cummins was now in charge of proceedings. That was when the proverbial hit the fan. John Kirkpatrick had Belinda in his ear every day, wanting to know why they weren't treating Rachel as a suspect. He told her they had considered whether the murder was carried out by a professional rather than a local with a grudge. They hadn't dismissed it out of hand, but several things didn't add up, so they shelved it until new evidence surfaced."

"The timing you mentioned didn't add up, guv," said Alex. "A hitman would have shot Gerry the second he was on the doorstep, not stand around arguing the toss for almost a quarter of an hour."

"Whoever it was," said Neil, "they carried a gun to the house. They were prepared to kill, but the extended conversation could suggest they went to negotiate, not assassinate."

"Negotiate what, though, Neil?" asked Blessing. "Gerry Hogan ran a successful business giving financial advice to fellow professionals. The vague description of the man on the doorstep didn't sound like the sort of person Gerry Hogan would represent, even allowing that it was a Sunday evening. But, as my father says, there's casual, and then there's casual."

"What type of gun was it, guv?" asked Luke.

"A semi-automatic pocket pistol," said Gus. "A Beretta Tomcat."

"How do we know that?" asked Luke.

"It turned up in the autumn of 2012," said Gus. "Matthew Knight, a local councillor, got fed up with local people moaning about drains getting blocked by falling leaves and standing water on several roads across the Common. After a phone call and a flea in the head of the Environmental Protection Department's ear, a road sweeper visited Trowle Common and cleared the drains and gullies. It was common for the sweeper operator to find shoes, coins, mobile phones, and watches. When he spotted the small gun drop out, he thought it was a novelty cigarette lighter. It wasn't much bigger than the palm of his hand."

"How far from the house was the gun found?" asked Alex.

"Over a mile," said Gus. "Yes, questions were asked why they hadn't found it in May. John Kirkpatrick had limited resources, and as each day passed, the trail grew colder. They confined the search area to several hundred yards around the property. Finally, the Beretta went for a forensic examination and proved to be the murder weapon. There were no fingerprints. The pistol had sat in a drain for five months, and every criminal worth his salt removes every trace of DNA before discarding a weapon."

"So, the detectives had a body and the murder weapon," said Lydia, "but no motive."

"That about sums it up," said Gus. "I reckon we should call it a day for today. We start looking for that motive in the morning."

Chapter Three

GUS GLANCED at the clock on the office wall as he headed for the lift. It was half-past four. He hoped the others made full use of the extra free time. Gus had a feeling they were in for a tough week.

The drive home to Urchfont wasn't as painful today. Gus tried to forget that he could be in the sweet spot between the end of the school run and the commuter crush by leaving thirty minutes earlier each day. Fat chance of that happening.

When he drew up in front of Tess's climbing roses, he remembered his first task once he got indoors. A hunt for their Last Will and Testament. Suzie wasn't home yet. He had thirty minutes at least before she made it here from London Road.

Gus collected the mail from the doormat and laid it on the hallway table. A glance told him it was mostly junk mail and letters re-directed from Worton Farm. He laid his jacket on the back of a chair in the kitchen and wondered where to start.

The logical place was most people's main bedroom, but Tess had a system. If it wasn't going to get looked at again, like the free local newspaper, it went straight into the recycling bin. For example, if she or Gus received a letter that referenced a date for an appointment or an event they wanted to attend, the details went on the kitchen's His and Hers calendar. The letter and its envelope could then get shredded. In due course, the contents of the shredder were transferred to the recycling bin.

Gus went along with this draconian system because it dramatically affected the amount of rubbish the couple gathered. From visits to witnesses' and suspects' homes, he knew only too well that people hoarded all sorts of items. They barely had room to move, and because there was so much trash, they couldn't find a blessed thing.

Gus had let the system slip since Tess died. He had ditched the His and Hers calendar and made sure that whichever type he bought as the New Year dawned had enough space each day to record appointments and notable events in his social calendar.

His hand hovered over the door handle, and he tried to visualise the contents of the various drawers and cupboards in the main bedroom—a large brown envelope with antique lettering, something that looked official. Gus was sure he would have seen it in the past few months, especially since Suzie burst into his life. Of course, Suzie wasn't always hoovering and polishing every spare minute, but she did help to keep the bungalow neat and tidy.

As Suzie searched for places to stow her bits and pieces, she would mention seeing a drawer or a shelf that she might put to better use. Gus soon reasoned that there was one place that Suzie would have left undisturbed. The dressing-table drawer in the spare bedroom. The room he would soon have to start calling the nursery.

He and Suzie had stood in the spare room at the weekend and discussed how to redecorate it. Something more practical and modern would replace the old dressing table. The full-sized bed had to disappear. Gus opened the drawer and a hint of Tess's favourite scent, Chloe, escaped into the atmosphere.

Gus had never gotten around to throwing away the personal items that retained so much of his memories of Tess. So when Suzie had told him she was moving in, he'd transferred them to the spare bedroom. He hadn't wanted Suzie to feel that he was clinging to the past and not committing himself one hundred percent to their relationship.

Suzie was the only person to have slept in that back room since he'd moved here from Downton. So when he switched the drawer's contents from the main bedroom, he thought the items would remain undisturbed for decades. Little did he know it would get used in a few months for a new arrival.

Gus opened the drawer and removed the chiffon scarf Tess had treasured that he'd used to cover her things. He picked up the brush that still held strands of her greying hair. He ran his fingers over the necklace he'd given Tess on her thirtieth birthday. Was it time to let them go?

Gus remembered when he'd returned home, and someone had trashed the place. The gangsters who murdered poor Frank North had left Gus a message. The police found an Order of Service printed with his computer and printer on top of this chiffon scarf. That death threat letter was no longer here. The police had entered the document into evidence.

What else lay in this drawer before he'd pushed it to one side to make room for Tess's possessions? Gus studied the fronts of several hard-plastic folders that Tess must have stored here for safekeeping. Put out the flags! According to Tess's handwriting on the label, he'd found one that carried the deeds to the bungalow, their will, and Gus's commendations and awards.

What possessed her to keep that rubbish, thought Gus. He grabbed the will and closed the folder on the Long Service and Good Conduct awards, the Chief Constable's Commendations, the Certificates of Excellence, Certificates of Recognition, and Bravery Awards.

Gus made a mental note to check what Tess had determined was worth preserving in those other file folders. That would have to be soon because the dressing table would be bound for the recycling centre or burnt in the back garden.

The BMD folder probably contained hatch, match, and dispatch certificates that covered the relevant ones for him and Tess, their parents, and possibly their grandparents. Family history was one area where Tess's draconian system didn't apply. She'd kept everything.

The sound of Suzie's VW Golf arriving on the driveway interrupted his trip down memory lane. With the large brown envelope securely tucked under his arm, Gus ventured outside to greet her.

"Hello, darling," he said. "Welcome home."

"Are you okay?" asked Suzie. "Did you only work half-day today?"

"Cheeky," said Gus. "We reached a sensible point to call a halt after giving our new case the once-over, so I sent everyone home thirty minutes early."

"What on earth have you got there," she asked, nodding

at the envelope. "It looks positively archaic. Is that papyrus, or vellum?"

"It's my will," said Gus. "Or at least, it was how things stood three and a half years ago. I've never revisited it to bring it in line with my changed circumstances. Don't take this the wrong way. I haven't had a note from the Grim Reaper telling me my time is almost up, but I need to be sensible at my time of life."

"You are a treasure, Gus Freeman," said Suzie as they walked indoors together. "Can I have first dibs on your vinyl collection? It would be good to get it in writing."

"I'm glad to see you're taking the matter seriously," said Gus. "Time can be short. Our latest victim, cut down in his prime at fifty-four, demonstrates that to great effect. I'm a few years older, but we had things in common. He was a successful professional with no enemies. He had a beautiful young partner and two teenage sons from an earlier marriage. On a pleasant Sunday evening, he stepped outside his front door to speak to someone, and that was it. Bang!"

"I'm going to shower and change," said Suzie. "I suggest you don't wander around the house with that document under your arm all weekend. Instead, find somewhere safe to stow it until you can give it your undivided attention. I'll make myself scarce on Saturday morning for one of the last occasions until after the baby's born. Why not have a crack at updating the contents when I'm absent? I'll gladly read it through with you in the afternoon. Unless you have other plans?"

"We need to clear the dressing table drawers in the nursery," said Gus. "The sooner we can empty the bedroom to give us scope for your planned refurbishments, the better."

"We do have time before that becomes urgent, Gus,"

said Suzie. "Don't forget what happened to Melody Davis. She and Neil had everything ready for the baby, and stress brought on a miscarriage. Let's take things a day at a time."

"Let's pray there's not a murder in the family to raise our stress levels then," said Gus.

Gus carried the envelope to the lounge and looked for a suitable spot. He slipped it onto the end of the rack of vinyl albums. He'd get a reminder every time he hunted for a record to accompany his musings about a case that there was something he'd forgotten to do.

Suzie returned, refreshed, and dressed in casual clothes. Her hair fell loose on her shoulders.

"That's better," she sighed. "I feel human again once I've got my uniform into the wash basket or the wardrobe."

"I'm not sure the about-to-be-crowned Chief Constable will appreciate one of his senior detectives considering the uniform made her inhuman," said Gus.

A cushion hit him in the small of the back as he headed for the bathroom.

"Don't take all night in there," said Suzie. "Although I have a lousy start to my days, it doesn't affect my appetite in the evenings. Thank goodness."

"If you're twiddling your thumbs while I shower, " Gus said, "you could phone the Lamb and book a table."

Gus rejoined Suzie fifteen minutes later.

"Are we good?" he asked.

"Despite everything," she said, "yes, we are."

"I meant for a table at the Lamb," said Gus.

"They never refuse me," said Suzie. "I threaten to wear my uniform the next time I'm in the pub. That seems to do the trick. We have your favourite table by the window, by the way."

Gus held out a hand, inviting Suzie to join him. She

made a meal out of levering herself off the settee and closing the three-yard gap.

"Just practising, darling," she said.

They left the bungalow and walked along the lane arm-in-arm.

"If you're hungry," said Gus, "you can have a starter, main course and dessert tonight."

"Are you sure we can afford it?" asked Suzie. "We have extra expenses ahead."

"True," said Gus as he opened the pub door, "but I'll save a fortune now you're on soft drinks for the next seven months."

As soon as they got inside, Gus heard a familiar voice.

"Evening, Mr Freeman and Miss Ferris."

Bert Penman was sat on his usual stool by the bar. That was where Gus expected to see him most nights before Irene North entered the equation. There was no sign of Frank North's widow this evening.

"Bert's a tad squiffy," whispered Suzie.

Gus had to agree. It appeared Bert had sat on that bar stool for a considerable time.

"Irene not with you tonight, Bert?" he asked.

"The Reverend is visiting her in the hospital," said Bert. "Irene is suffering from a nasty bout of food poisoning."

"Oh, we're sorry to hear that, Bert," said Suzie. "When did this happen?"

"The Reverend called the ambulance to Irene at lunchtime today, Miss Ferris."

"Will you be visiting her tomorrow, Bert?" asked Gus.

"I'm not sure it's my place to do that, Mr Freeman. People might talk."

"You and Irene have become good friends," said Gus. "Apart from the Reverend, who else in the village will drop in on her? A few of her older friends aren't in the best of health, and public transport isn't what it was. I'm sure that Brett will drive you there and back tomorrow evening. If push comes to shove, Suzie or I can arrange something."

"That's very neighbourly of you, Mr Freeman," said Bert. "I haven't troubled the hospital with my presence very often. But I remember my Cora saying the days felt more like forty-eight hours long when she was stuck in the Royal United for days."

"Will Brett be in later?" asked Suzie.

"It depends on when he returns to Urchfont with the Reverend," said Bert.

The landlord caught Suzie's eye. Their table was ready.

"We'll leave you to finish that pint of cider, Bert," said Suzie. "We're going to order a meal, and I expect you'll be getting off home."

Bert looked at the small amount left in his glass.

"They're not closing early, are they?" he asked.

Gus shook his head. Bert wasn't going to change his ways, not for Irene or anyone else.

Suzie examined the menu and the specials board.

"I can't decide what to have," she said.

"I'm having steak," said Gus, "followed by sticky toffee pudding. I'll get the drinks while you come to a decision. A large glass of Merlot and orange juice and lemonade coming up."

"You're not helping, Gus Freeman."

"I am trying," said Gus. "I've just spotted Clemency Bentham through the crowd. Brett won't be long behind her. Would you prefer we eat alone tonight?"

Suzie nodded.

"Ask after Irene and tell Clemency to pass on our good wishes."

Gus threaded his way back to the bar and spotted Clemency chatting to Bert. She gave Gus a wave. While Gus was waiting for his drinks order, Brett Penman tapped him on the shoulder.

"We've just returned from a visit to the RUH," he said. "Did you hear about Irene from Grandad?"

"We did," said Gus. "Suzie and I are dining over there by the window. We'll catch you later. How was Irene feeling tonight?"

"Rough," said Brett. "They know it's food poisoning, but they're not sure what caused it. I have my suspicions."

"By definition, it had to be something she ate," said Gus.

"Or the culprit was an ingredient Irene put into one of her cocktail recipes," said Brett. "I think Bert is drowning his sorrows over there because he grew the fruit or vegetable that Irene experimented with and feels guilty."

"That may explain why he seemed reticent about visiting her in the hospital," said Gus.

"Did he?" laughed Brett. "I'll get Clemency to gang up on him with me. She can't visit Irene every day. There are several parishioners in greater need at present."

"Clemency did mention that she would soon be writing a handful of her little speeches for visits to the crematorium," said Gus. "I'm always nervous when the Reverend has a clutch of funerals."

"I haven't heard this one, Gus," said Brett. "Does Clemency have form?"

"The Reverend certainly went up in Irene's estimation when describing Frank's past accomplishments," said Gus. "Clemency got the details that she'd scribbled down on her home visits mixed up with another chap from the village. As a result, Frank became a well-known sportsman and respected by all who met him, something that couldn't have been further from the truth if the Reverend had tried."

"I'll keep that one to myself, Gus," said Brett, "I'm sure Clemency has improved."

Gus picked up the tray containing his drinks order.

"I know she has, Brett," said Gus. "I remember hearing a junior doctor saying that even with training, it was tough to break bad news to a patient or their family members. They listened to senior doctors, and consultants go through the spiel with compassion and finesse and wondered whether they would ever get to be like that. I told the young doctor that it was the same for me as a young constable in Salisbury. My old sergeant sent me to tell the parents of an eighteen-year-old motorcyclist that he'd wrapped his bike around a tree and was never coming home. I was petrified. I made a terrible hash of it. I was almost in tears when I reported back to the station. He told me I'd get better at it if I stayed in the job for thirty years and had to do five hundred of them as he had. That young doctor got the message. Practice makes perfect."

"We vets have to cope with that dirty job too, Gus," said Brett. "Pet owners can get every bit as attached to their animals. Telling them that it would be kinder to put Fluff to sleep is a tough ask, as you say. Suzie's waving, by the way. I think they've delivered your food. You'd better get over there before it gets cold."

"Suzie must have found something on the menu she could eat at last," said Gus.

"Someone else with a dicky tummy?" asked Brett, looking at the tray's contents. "Or are you on the wagon?"

"Suzie's fine. She just wanted a clear head in the morning."

"I see. Well, we might not see you later," said Brett.

45

"Clemency has just prevented Grandad from sliding off his bar stool. My quiet drink might get curtailed if we need to take him home."

Brett headed to the other end of the bar to assist Clemency while Gus rejoined Suzie.

"Sorry it took so long," he said, "Brett was filling me in on Irene's condition. He suspects a dodgy cocktail recipe caused her to end up in the hospital. Remember the gin-laden cordial that gave her and the Reverend rosy cheeks?"

"Irene does enjoy an experiment," said Suzie. "Let's hope she's soon on the mend."

"My steak looks just how I like it," said Gus. "I can't wait to tuck in."

"I decided on the mushroom risotto, as you can see," said Suzie. "Nearly everything else on the menu had alcohol somewhere in the description."

"Brett spotted the soft drink," said Gus. "We won't be able to keep it a secret for much longer."

"I'm holding off until my twelve-week scan," said Suzie. "Mum and Dad won't say a word until we give them the green light. We'll tell Brett, Clemency, and the others when the time's right."

"Fair enough," said Gus. "what will you have for dessert?"

"I told the waitress we'd have two sticky toffee puddings," said Suzie. "A girl can only be a saint for so long. I didn't see any mention of alcohol in the ingredients, and for tonight I'll ignore the massive calorie count."

When Gus settled the bill, there was no sign of Bert Penman or his entourage. Brett had persuaded his grandfather to go home before the landlord chucked him out. He and Suzie made their way up the lane to the bungalow.

"It made a change to eat out on a Monday night," said Suzie. "I don't think we should make a habit of it, though."

"I agree," said Gus as he put the key in the front door. "I'll cook tomorrow evening. So start thinking about what you want now, and let me know when you make breakfast in the morning."

"Anything but mushroom risotto," said Suzie.

Tuesday, 14 August 2018

GUS WAS first out of bed in the morning. The alarm trilled at seven o'clock, and he was standing in the shower by five minutes past. He got dressed and checked that Suzie was getting up.

"How are you this morning, sweetheart?" he asked. Suzie growled.

"I'll make breakfast," said Gus, "If you feel hungry when you've visited the bathroom, let me know, and I'll rustle up something."

"Ugh, food, no thanks. Coffee for me, please, darling," said Suzie.

Gus resisted the temptation to reach for the bacon and eggs in the fridge. He opted for cereals with yoghurt instead of milk and scattered half a dozen raspberries on top. It wasn't haute cuisine, but healthy, and the smell wouldn't turn Suzie's delicate stomach.

He wondered how poor Irene North was feeling this morning. She might be better than Bert Penman after his long night on the cider. That stuff could be lethal. Suzie came out of the shower and returned to the bedroom to change into her work clothes.

Gus poured himself a second cup of coffee and one for Suzie. He strolled into the hallway to take another look at the post on the table. As he thought, three letters for Suzie and the rest could go in the bin.

"Was that for me?" asked Suzie as she came through to the kitchen. "I didn't take a close look last night. It was unlikely to be urgent."

Gus handed her the three envelopes and discarded the junk mail.

"A reminder from the dentist that I have an appointment next Thursday," said Suzie. "As if I'd forget. My membership with the Avon Valley Hunt needs to be renewed by the end of the month, and a bank statement. I need to notify those three people of my change of address. I ought to have done the lot in one fell swoop as soon as I moved in rather than ticking them off one-by-one when they make contact."

"I should remind you, miss, that failure to notify the DVLA of your change of address is an offence," said Gus. "You're lucky because I'm not an officer of the law. Ah, but you are - awkward."

"I knew there was a reason why I needed you," said Suzie. "Will you help me make a list tonight of the things that need attention?"

"Of course," said Gus. "You can make a start while I'm cooking dinner."

"I have a deep craving for cheese omelette and chips," said Suzie.

"Your wish is my command," said Gus. "Do you want a second cup?"

"No thanks, I'm good to go."

Gus grabbed his jacket from the chair and checked the car keys were still in the pocket.

"I'll see you tonight then, sweetheart," he said.

Suzie straightened her tie, checked in the hallway mirror that her hair was neat and tidy, and they left the house.

Suzie led the way along the lane, and they drove into Devizes in convoy. Gus wondered what this journey would be like in the New Year when he had to do it alone. There was no sign of Vera Butler walking to work this morning as he passed the London Road entrance.

Suzie raised a hand as she slowed to turn right to enter the car park, and Gus flashed his headlights. Something was reassuring about seeing the lights reflected in the back of her Golf. The windows were always an issue with his old Focus, but at least the lights never failed him.

Gus drove into town and passed the Crook Way junction to the new police building that had replaced their current accommodation. Gus missed the old Victorian buildings. They had character and were more of a deterrent in the middle of town than on the outskirts, no matter how smart the buildings might look.

The team had arrived before him, even though it was only ten minutes to nine. Everyone was keen to get started on the Hogan case. Gus travelled up in the lift and hoped they caught a break and found something that would offer a fresh lead to follow.

"Good morning, each," he said. "Luke, give me a name."

"Nick Barrett, guv. He's expecting you in his office at ten o'clock."

"Is he now? Where does he work, anyway? Barrett was at school with Gerry Hogan, wasn't he? Is he in the same line of business?"

"Nick Barrett was more than an old school chum, guv," said Luke. "They spent time together before Hogan married. Barrett was the best man at his wedding. Barrett's head of a law firm these days."

"Who do you want to ride shotgun, guv?" asked Neil.

"I reckon you deserve a crack at this one, Neil," said Gus. "Alex will be knee-deep in Gerry Hogan's business dealings for a few days."

"I'll drive us to Bradford-on-Avon, guv," said Neil.

"You don't need to leave for ages, Neil," said Lydia. "It's only a fifteen-minute drive."

"Is there something we can do in the meantime, guv?" asked Neil.

"You can put a date in your diary," said Gus. "I think we're overdue a night out at the Waggon & Horses, don't you? Everyone put in a good shift last week on the Duncan case. Shall we say nine o'clock on Friday night?"

"No problem, guv," said Neil. "Melody will enjoy a night out. Was there anyone else we should invite?"

"Who did you have in mind?" asked Gus.

"Rick Chalmers helped me out when the rest of you worked on the Ivan Kendall murder, guv," said Alex. "It would have taken longer at the Hub on that other business if I'd been working alone."

"Can I invite Divya, guv?" asked Blessing.

"I suppose so, Blessing," said Gus. "I don't know where Rick's working at present. He could be unavailable if he's working undercover."

Gus hoped that was the case. None of the team knew Kassie Trotter's spicy gossip about Rick and Vera Butler. If Rick turned up with Vera on his arm, that could make for an awkward evening.

"If you can get hold of him, and he'll be there, just let me know in advance," he said. "I don't want to have to borrow money from one of you to get the first round in."

Ten minutes later, Neil could sense that Gus was itching to get on the road to Bradford-on-Avon. No matter how long they'd hang around outside the law firm's offices before Nick Barrett invited them in.

When they reached Neil's car and were seated, Gus told Neil to wait before starting the engine.

"What did you make of Nick Barrett's statement, Neil?" he asked.

"Not sure I recall it word-for-word, guv," said Neil, "but the gist of it was that Gerry Hogan knew that his future lay in financial affairs from an early age. Barrett saw him as someone who would never get caught drinking underage, go shoplifting, or mix with the wrong crowd. He said that Gerry did his utmost to steer clear of trouble."

"What did the tone of that statement tell you about Nick Barrett?" asked Gus.

Neil started the car, drove slowly out of the car park, and turned left towards the river.

"We know that Barrett's a lawyer," said Neil, "I imagine he went into the profession straight from university. So, he's well-educated, aged around sixty, still living in the same town where he went to school."

"Did you check what type of law he handles? Family law, perhaps? Did his firm help draw up the will that Gerry's sister, Belinda, considered challenging?"

"I don't think so, guv," said Neil. "It's mostly employment law and personal injury claims that the firm of Barrett, Atkins, & Flook handle."

"I reckon the station car park will be closest to the firm's offices, Neil," said Gus. "Do you know where you're going?"

"I've driven here once or twice, guv," said Neil. "The Tithe Barn's worth a visit, and Melody and I strolled along the canal one Sunday afternoon last year when the weather was fine. We sat and watched a barge negotiating a lock. Always good for a laugh when the people who hired the barge don't have a clue what they're doing."

Neil parked the car near one of the large car park ticket machines. He studied the board through the windscreen.

"We're not likely to be here for much more than an hour, are we, guv?" he asked.

"Pay enough to cover us for four hours, Neil," said Gus. "You can claim it back on expenses. I want to sit and listen to what Nick Barrett says."

Neil knew Gus Freeman better than to query his methods. He was riding shotgun on this trip, clearly with nothing else to do but listen. Any questions he might have had in mind would have to wait until Gus gave him the nod.

They walked past the indoor swimming pool, where excited and raucous sounds suggested that dozens of local children were enjoying a morning dip as part of their school holidays.

Two minutes later, they were walking on Head Street and looking for the firm of Barrett, Atkins, and Flook.

"Here we are, guv," said Neil. "It looks like it's been here for a few years, doesn't it?"

"Established in the 1920s according to the brass plaque at the side of the door," said Gus. "Joseph Barrett would be Nick's grandfather, I presume. Nicholas followed in his father's and grandfather's footsteps. I wonder when Atkins and Flook became partners?"

Neil and Gus stepped inside the hallway. Stairs led to the first floor, and signs on the wall informed the newcomer that Mr Bruce Atkins was in Room Two, while Ms Natalie Flook occupied Room Three. Clients could also find Unisex toilet facilities located on the first floor.

Neil rang the bell attached to the wooden ledge in front

of a glass partition separating the hallway from an inner sanctum. Behind the glass, Gus could see two female members of staff. Both looked to have been with the firm since Nicholas Barrett was young. A white-haired lady studied them over her glasses. Her grey-haired colleague turned her head to join her.

Gus checked his watch. Two minutes to ten. What was their problem? Any idiot could work out that Mr Barrett was in Room One, where else, and on the ground floor. Gus marched along the corridor. The left-hand side of the partition slid open two seconds later.

"Do you mind? You haven't confirmed who you are and what business you have on these premises."

Gus turned back to see that the white-haired lady possessed a voice that could cut glass.

"Detective Sergeant Neil Davis, Wiltshire Police, ma'am," said Neil, showing her his warrant card. "Mr Freeman and I are here to talk to Nick Barrett. Our appointment is at ten o'clock."

"Does this Mr Freeman have a warrant card that I can examine?"

Gus showed her his consultant's card.

"That looks more like a library card. Are you sure you two are together?"

"Mr Freeman is my boss, ma'am. Can we get to Mr Barrett's office now, please? We know that time is money in your game."

"It's far from being a game, young man,"

It appeared that the grey-haired lady went to the same finishing school as her colleague.

"I'll tell Mr Nicholas that you've arrived."

"I think he knows," muttered Gus.

It was only fifteen seconds but felt much longer before

the door opened at the end of the corridor, and Nicholas Barrett stood in the doorway and beckoned them forward.

"Please, come in. Times have changed, I'm afraid. We can't have just anyone barging in off the street. Solicitors at other firms around the country have suffered serious assaults in their chambers. Daphne and Suzanne act as our resident pit bulls. They retired from their posts as doctors' receptionists and moved here three years ago. We haven't had a scrap of trouble since. So sit, and make yourself comfortable. The girls will bring us refreshments in a few minutes."

Finding a seat wasn't an issue as half a dozen chairs were in the large office. However, comfort was another matter altogether. Nick Barrett had inherited an excellent facility with floor-to-ceiling windows overlooking the rear garden. Unfortunately, the fixtures and fittings owed more to Joseph, his grandfather, than the twenty-first century, although the substantial desk that kept the two detectives at bay did contain a laptop.

Nick Barrett didn't appear to be in a rush to get to the point of the meeting. Perhaps he was waiting for his girls to deliver the coffee and biscuits before getting to business.

Gus wasn't that worried. The breathing space gave him time to take in his surroundings. The clock on the left-hand wall had hung there for almost a century. The elaborate walnut case surrounded a dial that wouldn't have looked out of place on the railway station concourse they'd just left. Gus wondered whether the loud tick was part of the solicitor's bag of tricks.

Tick. One pound. Tock. Two pounds. It served to remind clients that the bill was rising all the time. He moved in his wooden chair to get comfy and failed. The door behind him opened, and Daphne and Suzanne entered. Where was Kassie Trotter when you needed her?

Bone china cups, what else? Saucers and spoons too. A separate jug of milk and a bowl of sugar cubes. Daphne was in charge of pouring the coffee. Suzanne was *hors de combat* and wore a wrist support. Gus hadn't spotted that under the sleeve of her cashmere cardigan in the inner sanctum. The grey-haired lady's role was to carry a tray laden with Bourbon and Garibaldi biscuits.

"Thank you, ladies," said their employer. Daphne and Suzanne left without making a sound.

The tick on the clock seemed to get louder as Nick Barrett stirred two lumps of sugar into his milky coffee.

"To business then, gentlemen," he said, sitting back in his chair.

"DS Sherman contacted you and informed you that we were taking a fresh look into your friend's death," said Gus. "I want you to tell me everything you remember about your good friend, Gerry Hogan."

"Where do I start?" said Nick Barrett.

"From the beginning, sir," said Gus, "and don't leave anything out."

Chapter Four

GUS KNEW they were in for the long haul. The man hiding behind the impressive desk enjoyed being the centre of attention. They could learn a lot by giving Nick Barrett free rein to talk about himself just as much as Gerry Hogan.

It was easy to read through a murder file and absorb details of the victim, the suspects, and the eye-witnesses, without getting behind the words on the paper and analysing the leading players' genuine character in the drama.

Gus wondered how Gerry Hogan, an intelligent, hard-working, faithful husband and partner, suffered a pompous prig like Nick Barrett.

"It's so long ago now, Mr Freeman," said Barrett. He took a bite out of a Bourbon and sipped his coffee. "We met at Fitzmaurice Grammar in September 1969. We remained in the top stream together for the next five years, although we weren't always in the same classes when choosing O-Level subjects. Gerry had already decided that the Sciences weren't his forte, and frankly, as he was hell-bent on finance as a profession, they were next to useless. We both studied Mathematics and English Language, of course. Gerry was more of an athlete than I and had other friends from the school football, rugby, and cricket teams, but we became friends. I invited him to my twelfth birthday party, and Gerry returned the favour eight weeks later. So it continued. Gerry and I both lived in the town. We bumped into one another at the youth club on Mason's Lane and cycled around the local villages watching the girls go by as the song said. We survived those awkward early teenage years, and when around a quarter of us returned to the sixth form to study A-Levels, Gerry and I found ourselves in the same common room. He chose Maths, Economics, and Geography, while I opted for History, English, and Geography. They couldn't keep us apart for the entire two years. Barrett and Hogan. Batman and Robin. We both got A's across the board. We put in the work and got our reward. I remember telling DI Kirkpatrick when I spoke to him six years ago that Gerry was like me. He had his heart set on a particular career, and nothing was going to stop him. There were always distractions from students who wanted to smoke, drink, and get up to mischief. They would have deflected us from our goal. Sometimes Gerry kept me on the straight and narrow, that's for sure."

"You didn't have the same reasons for wanting to achieve your goal, did you, sir?" said Gus.

Barrett finished a second Bourbon and picked up a Garibaldi.

"You see through me, Mr Freeman," he sighed. "I would have chosen the arts, music, drama, perhaps. But, my father sat in this chair, his father before him. I had no choice but to pursue a career in law."

"You both did exceptionally well in your A-Levels," said

Gus. "That must have opened more options in your choice of university. Yet Gerry went up the road to Bristol to study Business and Finance."

"Bristol is still in the top five UK universities to study Law, Mr Freeman. It wasn't a rash choice. Gerry and I learned to drive with the same instructor, bought cars from the same second-hand lot, and took turns driving backwards and forwards. That's not to say we didn't immerse ourselves in the undergraduate experience. We certainly did that. Not for the first time, Gerry came to my rescue when I was in danger of falling foul of the law."

"After graduating, did you come here to work with your father?" asked Gus. "Was there a room available for you upstairs?"

"This firm was in transition, Mr Freeman," said Barrett. "When my grandfather opened the doors here on Head Street, he covered anything and everything. Of course, legislation was quite different a century ago, and when my father replaced Joseph as head of the firm, he tried to adjust to the changing times. By the time I arrived here from Bristol, he had specialised. We still handled criminal cases in those days, but the crime rate in a small country town does not keep the wolf from the door. I could tell that our future looked bleak unless we modernised and specialised. My father and I disagreed, so when Gerry told me his plans after graduating, I was only too glad to accompany him on his travels."

"You went to Australia for a gap year together then?" asked Gus.

"We did, and what an eventful nine months that was," said Barrett.

"Perhaps you can tell us more in a moment, sir," said Gus. "What happened while you were away?"

"My father was part of the furniture here with Barrett's from the early 1950s, working alongside my grandfather. Joseph Senior passed in 1978 while I was at university. So, as you can see, Joseph Junior had only had a couple of years at the helm. He'd been in the shadow of his father for so long that when the full glare of the spotlight fell on him, it soon became apparent that he wasn't up to the task. Clients who had been with us for years moved elsewhere. Large companies closed as imports crippled our industrial base. The writing was on the wall. The firm was on the brink of collapse, and my father did the only thing he could. He invited Bruce Atkins to join the firm. Bruce is a very able chap in the industrial accident and personal injury field."

"Where there's blame, there's a claim," said Gus.

"A crude description of what Bruce does, Mr Freeman. We're not ambulance chasers like those on the other side of the Atlantic. When I returned from my backpacking adventure, I found the new partnership was a fait accompli. My father was in his mid-fifties and not in the best of health. I couldn't argue with the decision to adjust the range of services we offered, but I could see that Bruce was only a sticking plaster that would keep us afloat for two, maybe three years. I also saw that my father wasn't the right person to drive the firm's necessary changes. So I persuaded him to step aside so that I could search for another partner. One who specialised in another area that offered the possibilities of a steady income stream."

"Natalie Flook, I assume," said Gus.

"No, Natalie only became a partner ten years ago. Fergus Dillon occupied Room Three upstairs from the early Eighties until he retired."

"From what I can tell in the time I've been here, the

adjustments you've made appear to have worked," said Gus. "The firm is far healthier than when you took charge."

"One does one's best, Mr Freeman.

"We know Gerry Hogan returned from Australia weeks before Evelyn flew to join him. You were their best man, weren't you? Did anyone rush from the other side of the world to meet up with you following your adventures?"

"Look at me, Mr Freeman," said Nick Barrett. "Imagine how I looked in my early twenties. I was short, overweight, and ordinary looking at best. Gerry wasn't a blond Adonis, but he had a far higher strike rate with the females than I ever did. That was true in the youth club on Mason's Lane, the university campus, or any pubs and clubs in Bristol where students gathered to socialise. I tagged along on our travels to Australia and talked to dozens of girls on the same voyage of discovery, but when Gerry and I flew home, my powder was still dry."

"Does that mean there isn't a young Barrett in the wings ready to join the firm?" asked Gus.

"I found someone eventually, Mr Freeman. I was in my early forties; Ginny was three years younger. We have a daughter, Josephine, who has no interest in the law. I'm happy that she's following the path I craved. Josie is an accomplished musician with hopes of becoming an actress. A career in musical theatre could be where she makes her mark. Ginny and I will support her every inch of the way. Five more years and this place will have a new name on the letter heading. Bruce Atkins will find a bright young thing to join the partnership, and Ginny and I can grow old gracefully."

"Unlike your best friend Gerry Hogan," said Gus. "Tell us about that Australian trip now, Mr Barrett. When DI Kirkpatrick conducted his investigation six years ago, he couldn't find anyone who might have wanted to murder Gerry. So that killer had to come from somewhere in his past. I've studied the murder file in detail, and I can't see evidence of much digging into what went on in the months before Gerry met Evelyn on the beach at Bondi."

"At the end of February, we took the late-evening flight from Heathrow with Singapore Airlines and settled in for the fourteen-hour flight to Singapore. Gerry's father drove us from home. He knew my father had already issued instructions on what to do and what to avoid at all costs. Gerry's father just told us to have fun. Don't do anything I wouldn't do type of thing. We had a delay before we took the connecting flight to Darwin, but we landed in Oz after twenty-three hours of travelling. After we collected our bags and reached the arrival hall, we soon found a striking-looking girl waving a placard for a hostel on our list of potential places to stay. Thirty minutes later, we walked outside into blistering heat and got in a combi-van with fellow travellers for the brief trip to our digs. The place was rough and ready. It marked the start of a succession of hostels where we slept, except for the drunken nights we spent on a beach somewhere. Within a month, I'd done the things my father told me not to do at least once, except finding a girl short-sighted enough to have sex with me."

"Gerry was more successful, I take it?" asked Gus.

"I don't know what other friends did in those situations, Mr Freeman," said Nick Barrett. "We would visit a bar, start drinking Toohey's, and check out the talent. Gerry was always better at chatting up the girls than I was, so I carried on drinking while he tried his luck. When he found two girls willing to join us, I'd loosened up sufficiently to converse with whichever girl wasn't his target. When we spoke the next morning, he didn't discuss whether they'd had a splendid night or a disaster. Thank goodness. Gerry was an honourable man. He wouldn't brag about his sexual exploits, nor would he say anything disparaging about the young ladies in question. If you pressed me for a number of nights when Gerry didn't sleep in the same room as me or close by me on a beach under the stars, I'd say five or six. One of those nights was different. That was the night he met Evelyn. She was a beauty. I could tell from the get-go that Gerry was smitten. I hadn't planned to sleep on the beach that night, but after another scorching hot day, a series of barbies where a hundred travellers congregated, drinking, smoking dope, and singing until the early hours, I couldn't get up off the sand. I was wasted. I fell asleep next to an eighteen-stone New Zealander who must have drunk two cans to each can that I managed and didn't stir until dawn. I remember stepping carefully through the arms, legs, and heads of youngsters still asleep. Everyone had stayed right where they were that night. Gerry was at the hostel when I stumbled in. We were almost at the end of our trip. I was fed up with sand in my bum crack every day. He didn't want to fly home. Evelyn was all he talked about on the flights from Sydney to Singapore, then Singapore to Heathrow."

"Evelyn flew to the UK to join Gerry a month later," said Gus. "They married in a registry office and then lived in Clifton. What did you make of that?"

"I was just glad to be in Bradford-on-Avon," said Barrett. "Long hot baths, the comforts of home. I wouldn't have missed that trip for the world, but I was in the thick of it here, trying to steer the firm into calmer waters. I liked Evelyn. She was a lovely girl, perfect for Gerry, and they made a handsome couple. I was proud to be asked to be his best man."

"After they married and rented that place in Clifton, did you see much of them?" asked Gus.

"Alas, no," said Barrett. "I was surplus to requirements: a third wheel and a busy man. Gerry and Evelyn were making their way in their chosen careers too, and when they had spare time, they naturally spent it together. We didn't lose touch entirely, and when Gerry bought his place on Trowle Common and my godsons arrived, Gerry and I met up far more frequently. Evelyn stayed at home with the children. Gerry and I would play snooker in the club on Market Street. It was one sport where I could join in with him without embarrassing myself. Gerry loved the game, as I'm sure you have learned."

"Whose idea was it to include a games room into the extensions to the Trowle Common property?" asked Gus.

"Not Evelyn's, if that's what you're thinking," said Nick Barrett. "She was happy for Gerry to see an old friend. Evelyn wasn't the sort to keep her man tied to the home. Everyone needs a little space at times, don't they? Gerry popped into Bradford for a few frames of snooker and a beer with me. Evelyn went upstairs to her studio and worked on her wildlife portfolio while Sean and Byron slept in the bedrooms next door. After I married, Ginny was probably glad for a few hours of peace while looking after our infant daughter. Like you, Mr Freeman, I struggled to think of anyone who might wish Gerry harm. He avoided trouble in his teenage years; his behaviour in his business life was exemplary. Nobody had a nasty word to say about him. Gerry had a fine grounding in that regard working at Hargreaves Lansdown. I knew several of Gerry's neighbours on the Common. He was a good neighbour, too, and never fell out with anyone. That was Gerry; he always wanted to be seen as doing the right thing, not attract any dirt that might stick to him and cause problems later in his life. Gerry didn't deserve to lose Evelyn as he did when she was doing something so worthwhile. Why do bad things happen to decent people? Then he found Rachel, and Ginny and I were pleased for him. He had a second chance to find happiness. When I heard about the shooting, it devastated me. Gerry Hogan was one of the finest men I've ever met. I miss his company."

"Did you keep in touch with Sean and Byron?" asked Gus. "As their godfather?"

"A different generation, Mr Freeman, and a tricky situation. Belinda started throwing accusations around like confetti after the contents of the will got made public. We didn't deal with that document. Gerry used a smaller firm on Market Street. Rachel was the major benefactor. Belinda received a lump sum, and Sean will get his inheritance next year when he reaches twenty-five. Byron has a further two years to wait. Rachel was less approachable than Evelyn. The snooker nights had reduced in frequency, partly due to Rachel, but Sean and Byron could play snooker with their father. Byron, more often than not, beat his father in the months before Gerry died. After Gerry's murder, it wasn't clear what might happen to the trio's living arrangements. Sean was eighteen, and Byron was sixteen. Rachel was a touch over thirty."

"Was there any talk?" asked Gus.

"When isn't there, Mr Freeman?" said Nick Barrett. "Far too many people have their minds in the gutter. Did the rumours have any substance? I didn't think so for one minute."

"How was the situation resolved?" asked Gus.

"Sean was due to go to university in September," said Nick Barrett, "while Byron should have started his A-Levels.

The boys lost their mother in 2002 and then their father ten years later. I wouldn't have been surprised if they rebelled after such tragedies. However, Gerry instilled the same standards of decent behaviour in his boys that I had admired for so long. Sean's A-Levels followed a similar path to his father's. He was destined to join his Dad in the financial services sector. Byron was less academic and took after his mother. Rachel had no interest in the business she inherited but was sensible enough to employ a manager to keep things running while Sean studied for his degree. No prizes for guessing where he studied. As for Byron, he is now a professional snooker player aiming to make it out of the Challenge Tour onto the World Snooker Tour circuit."

"So, we can find Sean running his father's old business," said Gus.

"Sean is still only twenty-four. Only a handful of the many thousands of financial services firms have over five employees. Many firms are run by just one person. Sean kept the services of Daniel Braund, Rachel's manager, and as far as I know, has no intention of flying solo in the immediate future."

"Is there anything else you think we need to know, sir?" asked Gus.

"Byron is in Turkey this week at a hotel in Antalya, playing in a tournament. Other than that, I have nothing."

"When was the last time you spoke with Rachel Cummins, sir?" asked Gus.

"Five years ago, possibly. I've had no reason to make contact. Sean Hogan plays snooker in the club that his father used. I see him there from time to time. It's Sean that keeps me appraised of Byron's progress."

"I think that's it for now, sir," said Gus. "We need to interview family members as soon as possible. Perhaps they will throw a chink of light on what happened six years ago. I must admit the whole thing has me baffled."

"Join the club, Mr Freeman," said Nick Barrett.

Neil and Gus left Nick Barrett behind his desk, looking out the window at the well-maintained lawn and shrubbery below.

"The bloke can certainly talk, guv," he said.

"That man is an expert at speaking at length and saying nothing that helps."

As Neil opened the front door and stepped back to allow his boss to leave first, Gus glanced through the glass partition into the inner sanctum. Daphne and Suzanne had stopped work and were staring straight at him. He gave them a friendly wave. They both stood up and made their way towards Mr Nicholas's office. Gus half-expected the glass barrier between them to become frosted.

"I hope they didn't expect to find any Bourbons or Garibaldis, guv," said Neil.

"I noticed you took advantage of not having any input in the conversation to fill your face, Neil."

"Did I miss the notice in the newspaper nominating Gerry Hogan for sainthood, guv?"

"Nick Barrett was a fan, wasn't he? Before he mentioned the wife and daughter, I wondered whether his interests lay elsewhere, despite the frequent references to females they met on the trip."

"I pegged him as an old-fashioned type, old before his time, guv. It goes with the territory. That legal language deliberately makes everything sound old and venerable."

"Did he mention one name we didn't already have on our list, Neil?" asked Gus.

"Not one, guv," said Neil, "apart from Ginny and Josephine. I can't see any point in interviewing them."

Gus and Neil returned to the station car park. The place was just as busy as it had been earlier.

"Five or six nights," said Neil.

"I made a mental note of that, Neil," said Gus. "Not sure how it helps us."

"No, I don't suppose those traveller hostels kept pristine records on who was staying there any more than they kept the rooms in five-star order."

"If we discovered that Gerry Hogan upset someone between February and November 1981, would that person wait until May 2012 before taking revenge? That's a non-starter, Neil."

As Neil drove them back through Holt village, Gus wondered what Alex had discovered. If Nick Barrett was right and Gerry Hogan was a saint, then that was another door slammed in their faces.

They were running out of doors.

"Where next, guv?" asked Neil as they entered the lift.

"Luke will have our next meetings arranged, Neil," said Gus. "Or he's for the naughty step. So please concentrate on Nick Barrett's background. Do some digging to determine whether he's the bumbling country solicitor he purports to be."

"Got it, guv," said Neil. "I can't see what Gerry Hogan saw in the bloke."

They exited the lift, and Gus headed for the restroom. Neil laid his jacket on the back of his chair and sat with a sigh.

"No joy?" asked Luke.

"Gus had a plan which didn't work for a change," said Neil. "I sat on my hands while Nick Barrett gave us his life story, with occasional references to our victim."

"What did you learn?" asked Blessing Umeh.

"In a nutshell? We got confirmation that Gerry Hogan was an honourable man in every part of his life. He was never in trouble and went out of his way to keep his friends on the straight and narrow. His business affairs will be squeaky clean, no matter how deep Alex digs, if we can believe everything his pal Nick says. Hogan's sons come from the same mould. During the gap year that Barrett and Hogan spent together, there were half a dozen occasions where Hogan may or may not have slept with a fellow female backpacker. As a gentleman, Barrett followed the line that he never discusses such matters; therefore, his pal Gerry would never say a word about what happened."

Gus returned from the restroom with two coffees.

"White, one sugar, Neil," he said. "Have you given them the potted version?"

"Pretty much, guv," said Neil.

"Any ideas where to look into Nick Barrett?"

"I can't talk to Bruce Atkins and Natalie Flook, guv. They're partners in the firm and will close ranks. As for the pit bulls in the office, well...."

"Daphne and Suzanne? I think we'll leave them well alone. They'll be very protective of Mr Nicholas. Your best bet is to do a spot of overtime one evening this week. Please drop by the club he mentioned on Market Street, and enquire about membership over a beer. Mention Barrett's name for a potential reference, then sit back and see the reaction."

"Right, guv. I can swing it with Melody once I tell her she's got a night out on Friday."

"What sort of club is it, Neil?" asked Lydia. "Are you sure Melody will let you go there?"

"It may have been a private members club in the past, Lydia. Perfectly proper and above board. The type of club where the only female they allowed worked behind the bar. I've visited dozens of them over the years. I imagine they were a welcome refuge for thousands of married men who just wanted somewhere to get away from their wives and kids for an hour between the wars and into the Fifties. Most places had a small bar, a dartboard, and a billiard table. Some termed themselves as Reading Rooms, which attracted teetotal men. They still had a billiard table, but the walls contained shelves of books and magazines rather than a dartboard."

"It sounds Victorian, guv," said Blessing.

"Most of the premises were from that era, Blessing. Now, who was likely to join such a club? Their membership came from middle-class professional men who avoided the working men's clubs like the plague—managers who didn't want to rub shoulders at the bar with the factory workers they employed. Everything changed in the Seventies when women insisted they should be allowed to join. A few famous golf clubs and London establishments held out for as long as possible. The result was inevitable."

"Quite right too, guv," said Lydia.

"Perhaps you should go to Market Street tomorrow night, Lydia, with Neil. Take a good look. When I joined the force in 1975, there were over a dozen similar clubs in Salisbury. I can show you three buildings within a hundred yards of this office that were once a hive of activity several evenings a week. Most had a small bar, a dartboard, and a billiard table. In the larger premises, there was also a skittle alley. You could argue that the type of club that only catered for men had had its day. But how many working men's clubs are still in business? Very few of the traditional variety. Times have changed. As an ex-copper, I know how valuable they were for obtaining information. I knew where certain people would be on any given night. I could drop by the Constitutional Club and find Billy Jenkins with a pint of Watney's Red Barrel in one hand and three darts with feathered flights in the other. A quick chat as he waited his turn at the oche, keeping as far away from the smoke from his Capstan Full Strength as I could, and I was on my way. If he gave me a useful tip, Billy found a pint behind the bar later, courtesy of the Salisbury Constabulary."

"My Dad worked that way too, guv," said Neil. "Terry hated the big family pubs that they built on the housing estates. They did away with the public bar, the snug, and the lounge. Everyone piled in together in one large room. The world and his wife could listen to your conversation, and he had no chance of spending a quiet five minutes with a source without someone spotting them. The villains squeezed the informants, and the sources dried up; sometimes, they closed down permanently. No, Dad was sorry to see the corner pub and those small clubs disappear."

"It is what it is," said Gus. "There's no way that way of life will ever come back. As for the club that Neil's going to tomorrow evening, they have two snooker tables and a bar," said Gus. "Barrett and Hogan went there regularly during their early twenties and less frequently when Hogan's family came along. These days, Sean and Byron Hogan are well-known in the club. After finishing work at the firm his father built, Sean plays a few frames for fun while Byron makes his name as a professional."

"The practice they put in at home must have paid off," said Luke.

"Every time I picked up a stick, it would remind me of the day my father got shot," said Blessing.

"A cue, not a stick, Blessing," said Gus, "but it's a fair comment. Gerry always played snooker once he added the games room to his home. The boys took to the game when they grew tall enough to reach the table. We'll learn how his death has affected them when we interview them."

"Byron Hogan is in Turkey this week, Blessing," said Neil. "Do you think we'll get a chance to fly out to interview him?"

"We'll concentrate on Sean Hogan and ask him when his brother returns to this country. I want to talk to Rachel Cummins first, anyway. What's the plan, Luke?"

"Tomorrow morning, guv," said Luke. "After nine o'clock. Ms Cummins's first fitness class isn't until the afternoon. Then she's at a gym in Bradford in the evening."

"Call her and say I'll be at her home on Trowle Common at nine-thirty," said Gus. "I'll drive here, collect one of you, and drive over."

Five faces looked from one to the other.

Who would get the short straw?

Chapter Five

"I HAVEN'T DECIDED who's coming with me yet," said Gus. "I need to reassess our strategy. Nothing is happening with this investigation. I thought by giving Nick Barrett enough rope, he might hang himself or at least reveal something damning about his best friend."

"Nothing works to fit the timeframe, does it, guv?" said Alex. "Hogan and Barrett were at school together...."

"And Bristol University," said Neil. "They took turns to drive there in term time and stayed in the city in the evenings enjoying student life."

"After graduating, they flew to Australia together," said Gus, "and backpacked from Darwin to Sydney via Alice Springs and Uluru."

"If one or both of them did something that made them a target, why did it take thirty years before someone sought them out?" said Luke.

"We can't dismiss the gap year entirely," said Gus. "But, again, if a jealous boyfriend discovered that Gerry Hogan slept with his girlfriend, fiancée, or wife thirty years before, it's a long time to hold a grudge."

"Maybe he slept with one of each, guv," said Neil. "They all chipped in for a hitman."

"Thank you, Neil," said Gus.

"Unless they had just discovered it happened, guv," suggested Blessing. "What if it was a couple who were married for the past thirty years, and things turned sour? Perhaps during the bust-up, the wife admitted she had cheated. The husband could have lost everything after the divorce, turned to the bottle for comfort, and started searching for the bloke his ex-wife had mentioned. He blamed Gerry Hogan for his miserable existence."

"What books do you read, Blessing?" asked Lydia. "That's a bit Mills and Boon, isn't it?"

"It's the only way I could bridge the gap between events in Australia and the murder six years ago," said Blessing.

"So, we *do* need to find out more about these liaisons Gerry Hogan had, guv," said Neil.

"Good luck with that," said Gus. "We can't ask Gerry Hogan. Nick Barrett doesn't have a clue, and the chances of the hostels they stayed at having records that go back that far are slim."

"There may be a way we can find the pieces of one of your jigsaws, guv," said Blessing.

"The famous jigsaws," laughed Neil.

"Go on, Blessing," said Gus. "Listen and learn, Neil."

"I'm not saying it would be easy, guv," said Blessing. "You say Nick Barrett knows nothing about the girls in question. That's not entirely true. What was he doing while Gerry was chatting up one of these girls earlier in the evening?"

"Sat in a bar somewhere, getting drunk," said Gus. Then he caught onto Blessing's train of thought. "Barrett told us he was chatting to her friend. That's our starting point. Get Nick Barrett to tell us about those girls. What part of the country did they come from, or were they local girls?"

"See if Barrett can recall which resort it was, which bar, and give us an approximation of the date," said Luke.

"First names would help," added Alex.

"What do we do with these scraps of information?" asked Neil. "We can't hope to trace them through hostel records. Airlines don't retain passenger records for long because of privacy concerns either, so we can't check who was in the country at the same time as Hogan and Barrett."

"Their trip was pre-internet days too, Blessing," said Lydia. "So, there won't be a pictorial record of someone's gap year on Facebook, unlike kids who have travelled Down Under in the past fifteen years."

"If I were travelling that far, I wouldn't go alone," said Blessing. "The person I chose to fly with would be a close friend. We would bond even more during the time away from home. I reckon those girls are still friends today, even if they're almost sixty years of age and living on different sides of the world. They're the sort of person who uses Facebook to keep in touch with old friends. If I had first-name pairings and places they visited, maybe Divya could write a search routine to find possible candidates."

"You needn't worry about upsetting one of them by asking if they knew a Gerry Hogan," said Neil. "According to Nick Barrett, Gerry went for the most attractive girl in the bar. It shouldn't be difficult to work out which one of the two he chose."

"It's a long shot, Blessing," said Gus. "At the moment,

though, I have got nothing better to suggest. We'll run with it for a couple of days."

"Wish I had the magic bullet, guv," said Alex. "I've only spent half a day so far studying the firm's website. They follow the traditional spiel for these sites. I don't know how much of what I can see is Sean's recent input, that of the manager Rachel Cummins installed in the interim or even Gerry's original concept for the business. You can confirm that when you interview them."

"Firms such as Gerry Hogan's are investing in your financial future," said Luke. "There's always a price to pay for that advice, plus none of them forgets to add the important rider. Always seek a professional opinion. Tax rules can be complex; they can depend on individual circumstances and are subject to change. The value of investments and the income from them can go down as well as up. Nothing is guaranteed. You might not get back your initial investment."

"Have you had personal experience?" asked Alex. "That sounded to be from the heart."

"Not me, but a shifty advisor royally screwed my parents. It's all very well warning people to seek professional advice. Even someone with the right diploma can be a scam artist or simply give you the wrong advice by not giving your account due care and attention."

"If we take Nick Barrett's comments at face value, then nobody suffered under Gerry Hogan's watch," said Gus.

"I didn't go directly to the Hogan website, guv," said Alex. "I did hunt for the dirt on them first. I didn't find anything. Nothing has been serious enough to make it to a court or the media."

"Follow the money," said Gus. "That's what they keep telling us. Something must turn up, Alex. It has to. Nothing that Nick Barrett told us this morning helped to explain why someone wanted to kill Gerry Hogan."

"Are you convinced Barrett is telling the truth, guv?" asked Lydia.

"If he was lying through his teeth, Lydia, he fooled me. Neil will put him under the microscope, but it's another long shot."

"What should we do, guv?" asked Blessing.

"Are you asking for a worthwhile task that might dislodge a clue?"

"As opposed to a general cry for help, yes, guv," said Blessing.

"Well, something you said about a possible chain of events in Australia is still nudging me in the ribs. It can't hurt to search for news items between the dates our intrepid explorers were Down Under. It might not be a spurned lover, just an incident that made it into the newspapers. You're looking for incidents where backpackers fell foul of the law or got on the wrong side of the locals. Check for sexual assaults, that sort of thing."

"Everything we've learned so far doesn't mark Gerry Hogan as a sexual predator, guv," said Neil. "He got more than his fair share anyway."

"We only have Nick Barrett's word for that," said Gus. "It's worth checking, especially when we have little else to go on."

"Nick Barrett told us he was unsuccessful the whole time he was in Australia," said Neil. "Perhaps he was hiding something."

"It still begs the question, Neil," said Alex.

"Why wait for thirty years," sighed Neil. "I know."

"And why kill Gerry Hogan if Nick Barrett was the guilty party?" asked Lydia.

"Unless they got the wrong man," said Blessing.

"The man on the doorstep asked for Gerry by name. So let's keep going with the lines of enquiry we started with," said Gus, "plus the items we've added this afternoon. We'll debrief what we've learned on Thursday morning and reassess if necessary. For the rest of what remains of today, I suggest we update our digital files and then head home. Tomorrow will be a better day."

Wednesday, 15 August 2018

GUS HAD ARRIVED home at twenty-past five last night and started cooking the meal he'd promised Suzie. He resisted settling for the cheese omelette and chips that she fantasised over. There were ample supplies of healthier ingredients in the fridge and freezer.

Suzie drove through the gateway at twenty minutes to six. Gus had a bottle of Chardonnay poised to pour her a glass and paused. Half a glass for himself while he finished cooking and a glass of water at the kitchen table when they ate. Old habits die hard.

"Did you make any progress with your case today, darling?" asked Suzie as she breezed through the hallway into the main bedroom.

"Two steps forward, three steps back," said Gus.

"Never mind. There's always tomorrow."

Five minutes later, Suzie joined him in the kitchen. She looked radiant.

"That smells good," she said. "You'll never guess who I saw going to lunch together today."

"Vera Butler and Rick Chalmers," said Gus.

"Heavens, no. Where on earth did you get that idea? They're the most unlikely pair I know. No, it was our police surgeon and the new girl."

"Rhys Evans and Grace Packenham?" said Gus. "I hope they stuck to the thirty-minute comfort break she imposed on the rest of the back-office staff."

"No idea; I spotted them walking along London Road as I moved between the Hub and the main building. Geoff Mercer has added another topic to the list of things he wants me to oversee. In a few weeks, I'll need to gently tell him that I won't be there to keep his string of plates spinning."

"What was it this time?" asked Gus.

"Victim support," said Suzie. "It's a good idea because it dovetails with the other projects I'm handling."

After eating, Gus joined Suzie in the lounge, where they tackled the list of people and companies she needed to notify of her change of address.

"Not an exciting evening," he said after they finished the task, "but worthwhile."

"Will tomorrow night be exciting then?" asked Suzie.

"I need to spend an hour or two at the allotment," said Gus. "August is half over, and I've got lots to do. If you feel up to it, you can come with me. Then we'll drop into the Lamb. I'd like to hear from Bert how Irene was this evening. Brett said last night that he was taking him to the RUH whether he protested or not."

"I'll see how I am," said Suzie. "I can rustle up that omelette and chips for us to enjoy. Then we could walk to the Lamb later. What have you got planned for the morning?"

"I have a nine-thirty meeting with a fitness instructor," said Gus. "A beautiful thirty-six-year-old single lady."

"Time for bed," said Suzie. Gus didn't argue.

They both got out of bed a few minutes later than usual in the morning. Suzie felt better than she had for a week, and they sat in the kitchen, eating breakfast together for a change.

"If this mood lasts throughout the day, I might join you at the allotment after all," said Suzie as they dressed, ready for work.

"Fingers crossed," said Gus. "Before I do a thing today, I need to decide who to take with me for this morning's meeting."

"Who is this woman you're seeing?" asked Suzie as they left the bungalow.

"Our victim's partner," said Gus. "They'd been together for five years. There was talk when she inherited most of his estate, but nothing suggests she had anything to do with his death."

"Is she still single?"

"I don't know," said Gus. "I don't remember reading her current status in the murder file."

"You didn't consider interviewing her on your own?"

"Geoff said that I should always have a serving officer present. We've strayed from that on the odd occasion. I vary the team member who comes with me for obvious reasons."

"To share the load and make sure each of them feels as important as the rest," said Suzie. "That should be standard practice, but I've met senior officers who do the exact opposite."

"Don't bite my head off, but Lydia has been the ideal choice when talking to male suspects or inmates. She distracts their attention from the line of questioning."

"There's a word for that, Gus Freeman."

"I think Luke might fit the bill today," said Gus. "Does that fall into the same category?"

"Possibly," said Suzie. "You might not learn as much from this woman if two blokes gang up on her. She might not suss that Luke's gay. So why not take Alex Hardy?"

"Alex is crunching the numbers for the financial firm our victim ran. I don't want to take him off that task. It's our last hope for a quick breakthrough."

"Luke, it is then," said Suzie. She got into her Golf and set off for London Road.

Gus followed her to the car park and drove to the Old Police Station office. Neil Davis was already upstairs when Gus exited the lift.

"Morning, guv," said Neil. "All systems go for today and tonight. I've cleared a visit to the snooker club with Melody, and Nick Barrett reluctantly agreed to see me at eleven-thirty this morning."

"Terrific, Neil," said Gus. "Press him hard for information on the girls with whom Batman and Robin chatted, whenever and wherever that was. Feed that to Blessing so she can liaise with Divya in the Hub. The sooner we can get those searches underway, the better. Good luck tonight, too. You might bump into Sean Hogan. If you do, then beat a hasty but dignified retreat. I won't have time to talk to him until tomorrow. I don't want him spooked by finding out we're digging into his family's background and Nick Barrett."

"Got it, guv," said Neil. "That sounds like the others coming up now."

Luke and Blessing were next to arrive.

"Luke, you're with me this morning," said Gus. "It's okay if you didn't bring your shorts and trainers. We'll talk to Rachel Cummins, not take one of her fitness lessons."

"Very droll, guv," said Luke.

The lift descended to the ground floor again, and Alex and Lydia came up and joined them.

"Everyone's here, and it isn't nine o'clock," said Gus. "That's what I like to see. You know what you've got to do, Alex. Neil's returning to Bradford-on-Avon later, and you two girls are scanning old news items. Luke and I will catch up on your progress when we return."

"We should get to Trowle Common bang on half-past nine, guv," said Luke as he and Gus headed for the lift.

"I don't mind making Ms Cummins wait," said Gus. "I'm more worried about this lift. It's up and down more than an assistant referee's flag."

Luke hesitated when they reached the car park.

"What's up?" asked Gus.

"I didn't want to presume that we were using my car, guv," said Luke.

"Jump in the Focus, then. What's life without the occasional risk?"

"Neil said his role in Barrett's office yesterday morning was to listen, make notes, and inwardly digest. Is that the same for me today?"

"If a reply from Rachel triggers a fresh line of questioning, don't hesitate. Go for the jugular. By the way, is Ms Cummins single?"

"I believe so, guv," said Luke.

"I guess we'll find out when we get there," said Gus.

Gus drove them through Trowbridge and onward to Trowle Common. They arrived outside the Cummins and Hogan property without mishap one minute before the appointed time.

"I couldn't have judged it better, guv," said Luke.

"Five sets of lights against us out of six, Luke. Judgement had nothing to do with it. I blame the Wiltshire Highways Department."

"It's an impressive property, guv," said Luke. "I wonder whether they've made further improvements since Gerry's death."

"Apart from a new driveway, d'you mean?" said Gus.

Luke studied the clean gravel at the front of the house. He would have moved if it were him. Every time he opened the front door, he'd see the body and the blood.

"Why did we leave the car back there on the road, guv? It's a fair walk to the house."

"Ms Cummins is a fitness instructor, Luke. I wanted to get off on the right foot. Anyway, there's a method to my madness. I want to see whether she can see our car from the front doorstep."

Gus stood on the doorstep and turned around.

"The trees and bushes screening the property from the road will have matured in the past six years. The road was more visible back then. There were very few places for that chap to park that obscured any motorcycle from view."

Luke rang the bell.

"I wonder if that's the same ring," said Gus. "A pint on Friday night says she bought a new one."

"No contest, guv," said Luke. "Do you think Rachel will open the door in her lycra outfit?"

"Odd place to have a door, Luke," said Gus.

Luke groaned.

"I've waited years to say that again," said Gus.

Rachel Cummins opened the front door wearing a fitted white blouse, high-waisted black trousers, and flat patent leather shoes. There wasn't a pair of trainers in sight, let alone lycra.

"You must be the police officers I'm expecting. Do come

in. I've got coffee on the go in the kitchen. If you go straight through, you'll find the sunroom. It's lovely there in the mornings. I'll be with you in a minute."

Gus and Luke did as instructed. The sunroom furniture was top-of-the-range, as expected. Everything about the property oozed quality. Gus wondered why Rachel Cummins didn't sell up and move into a smaller place in Bath. Something must make her want to stay out here in the sticks.

A door opened to their left, and Rachel Cummins reappeared with a tray.

"What does everybody want?" she asked.

Luke answered for both him and Gus. Rachel smiled.

"You know who I am," she said, "so, which of you is Detective Sergeant Sherman?"

"I'm DS Sherman, and this is Gus Freeman, a consultant with Wiltshire Police."

"How can I help?" asked Rachel.

"As Luke will have explained when he phoned you, Ms Cummins," said Gus. "We're taking a fresh look into the murder of your partner, Gerry Hogan. It might be six years, and the original investigation didn't reach any firm conclusions, but no murder file is ever closed. We hope to find Gerry's killer this time around."

"It made little sense," said Rachel. "Gerry didn't have an enemy in the world. It had to be random. The police went over this ground six years ago. I can't see how it will be any different."

"If we ask the same questions, we'll get the same answers, Ms Cummins," said Gus. "My team has had a fair bit of success in the past few months by listening to what people say and then asking a different question. Perhaps one that that person didn't expect. Their answers can be revealing."

"If I were guilty of any crime, that comment would put me on my guard, Mr Freeman," said Rachel, "but no matter what questions you ask, you will only ever get the truth. I had nothing to hide six years ago. Nothing's changed."

"You were born in Surrey in 1982, I believe," said Gus.

"My parents lived in Haslemere. Dad worked on the buses, and Mum worked part-time in a flower shop before I started school."

"Their marriage ended when you were eighteen months old," said Gus. "What do you remember of that time?"

"Not much," said Rachel.

"Did they argue? Can you remember them shouting? Was your father violent towards your mother? Did nothing register?"

"I remember Mum crying," said Rachel. "I didn't understand why. I still don't. She hasn't spoken to me about it. After Dad left, it was just the two of us. I never saw or heard from him again. It would be best if you asked Mum. Not that it's got anything to do with Gerry's murder. It was hardly front-page news; lots of marriages break down."

"Your mother didn't look for another man?" asked Gus.

"No, it was the two of us against the world. Mum started full-time in the flower shop once I started school. We were never flush with money, but we always got by. Mum and I holidayed in this country: Great Yarmouth, Southend, Bognor Regis, and places like that. We usually stayed on a caravan site. Cheap and cheerful. My grandfather died when I was seventeen, and my gran had passed a couple of years earlier. Mum used the small windfall from Granddad's will to pay for me to go through college,"

"You wanted to get the right health, fitness, and exercise diplomas to enable you to teach, I suppose," said Gus.

"More than wanted, Mr Freeman," said Rachel Cummins, "it was what I'd set my heart on ever since I was a young girl."

"At twenty, you carved out a career as a personal trainer. I imagine that was hard work?"

"It involved hours of preparation and miles of driving to and from village halls, gyms and fitness centres in a twenty-mile radius of Haslemere. I had the drive and determination necessary to be successful. After three years, I felt I'd cracked it."

"Your comment suggests that something threatened that success," said Gus.

"Was that when your mother found someone?" asked Luke.

"Lawrence Wallace, yes," said Rachel. "Mum knew him first when they were in secondary school. They went out together for three months. When my Dad moved to Haslemere from Guildford to live, that changed. Dad swept Mum off her feet, or so she said. What happened next was my fault. I bought a computer for my accounts and saw the potential for Facebook to help my business. Mum wanted to know what it was all about, and I showed her where several of my school friends had got in touch. The next thing I knew, Mum had an account and ten friends. Most were girls from her schooldays or work. Then she found her old boyfriend online. The next thing I know, he's on the settee when I get home from work."

"You didn't like him, is that fair?" asked Luke.

"He was a creep," said Rachel. "I dressed in a way that suited the work I did. I still do. He undressed me with his eyes. I couldn't stay in the house once he'd moved in, nor could I explain to Mum why I needed to find my own place. She was happy, and I didn't want to spoil things for her. I just knew he was the sort of bloke to try it on if I was ever alone with him."

"You experienced similar unwanted advances on home visits," said Gus.

"The old ones were the worst," said Rachel. "They couldn't touch their toes, but their hands found a breast or my bottom in milliseconds. They never scared me. I knew I was strong and fast enough to control the situation before it got out of hand."

"Why did you choose to move to Bath?" asked Gus.

"Most people have seen photographs of Bath," said Rachel. "It's a beautiful city. No way was I moving to London. A huge impersonal place with far too much competition in my line of business. I thought the average age of people in and around Bath would suit my approach to exercise. I knew it would take hard graft to create as good a circuit as I had in Surrey. The primary reason was that Bath was far enough away from Lawrence Wallace to dissuade him from popping round to try his luck."

"You moved home only after you had done your utmost to get your existing clients fixed up with an alternative trainer," said Gus. "I find that commendable."

"I couldn't leave them in the lurch. Some had been with me from the beginning."

"How did you avoid the clutches of your mother's new partner?" asked Luke.

"My evenings were spent working or visiting other trainers' sessions to see if they were willing to take on new clients. I didn't run any sessions on Sundays, so I drove to Bath, searching for a flat to rent and venues I could hire. I advertised in local papers and newsagents windows.

Anything to get the message out. It was slow to take off, but I got there."

"How long had you been working here before you met Gerry Hogan?" asked Gus.

"Two years. One of the first places I had on my list of venues was that place in Bradford-on-Avon. Every Thursday night, rain or shine. I still run sessions there now if you're interested."

"I play squash most weeks with my partner," said Luke, "and Mr Freeman spends several hours weekly on his allotment. We're fine. Thank you. There is one thing you've not mentioned when you covered the first twenty-three years of your life. Was there nobody in your life other than your mother? No boyfriends or girlfriends. No significant other. You are an attractive woman, Ms Cummins. I'm sure it wasn't only old men and lecherous male friends of your mother who took an interest."

"I had boyfriends at school and college, DS Sherman, but my focus was always on my career. Nothing was going to distract me from achieving my goal. I must admit that there was always the thought that I didn't want to make the same mistake as my mother in the back of my mind. From the age of twenty, when I started work as a personal trainer, I was too busy to stop and look for anyone."

"You must have socialised in that first two years when you lived in Bath," said Gus. "There's no shortage of places to go to meet new people. Would you have us believe you were too busy ever to take a break?"

"I didn't know anyone when I moved from Haslemere," said Rachel. "The only friends I had were among the new people that signed up for my fitness classes. Of course, most of them were women. Many were far older than me, but I found plenty of students and lecturers who needed to keep fit and healthy in a university city. I can honestly say that although I enjoyed their company whenever we met up away from the classroom, I didn't meet a man that sparked my interest. Perhaps I wasn't looking hard enough in the right bars and clubs. Instead, I visited the theatre and went to concerts and film shows in the Royal Crescent. It might sound boring, but I can assure you, I was happy with my lot."

"Then, one Thursday evening in Bradford-on-Avon, a forty-nine-year-old man signed up for you to get him fit again," said Luke. "Gerry Hogan walked into your life, and suddenly everything changed."

"Your line of questioning suggests that you have me marked down as a man-hater," said Rachel. "Because I was unhappy getting fondled on home visits; and imagined that Lawrence Wallace planned to attack me. That's rubbish. I should be able to visit men in their homes for an exercise class without them invading my personal space. Men like Wallace should understand the boundaries and respect them. He was dating my mother, for heaven's sake."

"I'm not sure our line of questioning was contentious," Gus said. "Gerry Hogan died outside his front door six years ago. You lived with him here for four years. If DI Kirkpatrick didn't dig deep into your history and relationships, then that was remiss of him. If the killer didn't come from Gerry's distant past, it had to relate to someone he'd recently met. DS Sherman was within his rights to ask why you changed after several years of celibacy."

"People say they don't believe in love at first sight, Mr Freeman," said Rachel. "All I can say is they've never experienced a night like that. After the session ended, I wanted to learn what Gerry wanted from the course. That's standard practice; I want my clients to get the most out of their time with me. As soon as we talked, there was an instant attraction. That had never happened with any other man I'd met during my working life. I couldn't wait for the following Thursday night to see him again. Gerry was vulnerable. He told me what had happened to his wife and how he'd brought up his sons alone. I told him about my home life and my career. Conversation flowed so easily that it felt like we'd known each other for years."

"That wasn't strictly true, was it?" said Luke. "Gerry had a good deal of help from his sister, Belinda. He couldn't have raised Sean and Byron alone and continued to develop his financial services firm."

"Belinda was a cow," said Rachel. "I'm sorry, but she was a bitter spinster who saw Gerry as a surrogate husband. Belinda treated those boys as if they were her flesh and blood. From the minute I met her, she did everything possible to drive a wedge between us. Gerry couldn't see it. He loved me, loved the boys, and we lived in this house for four wonderful years. Belinda couldn't stand getting shut out. When the will surfaced after Gerry's death, that was the final straw. Belinda started the rumour that I'd persuaded Gerry to change his will, then paid someone to kill him. Gerry didn't tell me much about the old will because it was none of my business. We were looking to the future. I was thirty, Gerry was over twenty years older, but we should have had another twenty years together, at least. There was no rush to make a will. We weren't married. Gerry had never asked me, but I expected him to ask one day, maybe once the boys got settled. I would have said yes because I loved him, and we were perfect together. It was ludicrous to suggest I wanted him dead."

And yet, someone did, thought Gus.

Chapter Six

"I DON'T WISH to go through every step of what happened that Sunday evening, Ms Cummins," said Gus. "I realise it was painful. Can I perhaps pose a series of questions to check that I have my ducks in a row?"

"I'll never forget what happened, Mr Freeman," said Rachel, "and I can't imagine that I'll tell you something different to what I told the detectives six years ago. Despite what you said earlier."

"We'll see," said Gus. "How did that Sunday differ from any other before six-thirty in the evening?"

"The boys didn't get up until lunchtime. That was normal. I was just as fond of my bed when I was that age. Gerry and I ate breakfast alone. He popped into town to get a few things from the supermarket while I cooked Sunday dinner. We ate in the evenings in the winter months, but from May to September, we ate earlier, so we had the rest of the day to do whatever we chose. That Sunday we ate at five o'clock. The boys and Gerry didn't want to drive to the coast or visit a country park that weekend."

"They were keen on snooker," said Luke.

"They played in the games room whenever they had the chance."

"Was the gym here when you moved in?" asked Gus.

"No. Gerry extended the ground floor to accommodate my gym and a bigger kitchen. That work finished six months after I came here."

"Did Gerry and the boys ever use the gym?" asked Luke.

"Gerry used it more than the boys. He didn't mind working out with me. Sean and Byron were teenagers, and their bodies were changing. They felt uncomfortable exercising with me. I never pushed it. They used the gym alone or together when I was away working."

"Did you exercise every Sunday evening?" asked Gus.

"Not if we'd had a long day out as a family, no," said Rachel. "Around that time, I was developing new routines that needed polishing before I could introduce them to my clients. You can't keep doing the same things forever. I wanted to freshen things up, and that Sunday was one of those occasions."

"You must have been annoyed at getting interrupted," said Gus. "Surely one of the boys could have gone to see who was at the front door?"

"Do you have teenage sons, Mr Freeman?" asked Rachel.

"I have not," said Gus.

"Sean and Byron wouldn't stop what they were doing to do something so mundane. Well, Gerry preferred one of the grown-ups to answer, anyway. He said you never knew who it was or what they wanted. So, when Gerry didn't respond, I decided I had better."

"You grabbed a towel, wiped yourself down, and dashed to the door," said Luke.

"What did you see?" asked Gus.

"A tall, white man, casually dressed, who was half-turned away from me."

"Like a cold-caller, who is half-expecting you to tell him you're not interested before he gets the chance to say what he's selling," said Gus.

Rachel laughed. Gus thought what a pleasant sound it made. It was easy to see why Gerry Hogan had fallen for her.

"Spot on. Mr Freeman. I hadn't thought of it that way before, but I thought he was a nuisance caller as soon as I set eyes on him. Nobody turned up on a Sunday evening without calling first. As I said, we went out as a family during the summer months."

"There was no chance you had ever seen the man before?" asked Luke.

"Never," said Rachel. "A total stranger."

"Were you surprised when he asked for Gerry by name?" asked Gus.

"Yes. He didn't look like a man that Gerry would know. Does that sound awful? Gerry was no snob, but most of his friends were professional men, if you know what I mean."

"Men similar to Nick Barrett, the solicitor, and the well-to-do clients that Gerry handled."

"Yes, Nick and Gerry went way back. He has a rather high opinion of himself, but Nick's harmless, bless him."

"You saw little of him, though?" asked Luke.

"Nick didn't visit while I was here. He might have done it while Evelyn was alive. Nick met her in Australia, too, of course. But, no, Gerry and the boys saw Nick regularly in

Bradford-on-Avon. They played snooker together at the club on Market Street."

"We've learned something new today," said Gus. "I told you we would."

"I don't follow," said Rachel.

"The police were searching for a tall, white, casually dressed man of indeterminate age," said Gus. "They should have added that the man's casual attire suggested he was of working-class origin."

"He *was* scruffier than Sean or Byron ever were, that's for sure," said Rachel. She was staring out of the sunroom window as if she was back on the front doorstep on May the sixth, six years ago. "His trainers were well worn, and he didn't tie the laces. He tucked them into the tops as lads did back then."

"Early to mid-twenties then," said Luke, "but certainly no older."

"I suppose so," said Rachel. "I don't know why that came back to me. I've tried to put it behind me."

"You only stood at the door for a few seconds," said Gus. "Did you wonder how he'd got to Trowle Common?"

"I didn't give it a thought," said Rachel.

"How did we get here today?" asked Gus.

"By car, I presume."

"It's parked a yard beyond the gateway, on the right. Could you see it from the door?"

"Only a blur. I wear glasses when doing paperwork, but I'm too vain to wear them at any other time. I tried contact lenses, but they irritated me too much. Why?"

"A neighbour heard a motorcycle leave the area at around six forty-five," said Gus. "If you had caught even a glimpse, you would have known it was something only a youngster would ride. When you matched that to the trainers and the man's general demeanour, you would have given DI Kirkpatrick a far more accurate description of the man."

"I wanted to get back to the gym," said Rachel. "I didn't know the man. I didn't know what business Gerry could have with him. My new routines needed practice, so I called Gerry and returned to the gym."

"Were you preparing these routines to music?" asked Luke.

"Yes," said Rachel.

"How did you hear the doorbell?" he asked.

"If you want the grand tour later, you can see what Gerry had installed. He rigged up a discreet security system in the principal rooms. Everywhere except the two bathrooms. An amber light shines when someone rings the doorbell. A green light shows the landline in the hallway. If we saw a red light, one of us had to call 999 because it meant burglars had broken in through an external door or window. When the doorbell rang, I had my headphones on, but I spotted the amber light flashing above the gym door."

"What about when Sean called for his Dad at a quarter to seven?" asked Gus.

"I had almost finished what I wanted to do," said Rachel. "I'd removed the headphones and was tidying away the equipment I'd used. Then, I heard Sean shout and wondered why Gerry hadn't got rid of that guy yet. So, I went through to the hallway and looked outside."

"What did you do next?" asked Gus.

"I screamed and ran outside to see if there was something I could do, but it was pointless. Gerry was dead. I saw Sean and Byron standing in the doorway, frozen in shock. I told Sean to go back indoors and phone the emergency services. It was a nightmare."

"When you first walked outside, did you see or hear anything?" asked Gus.

"The man had gone. I didn't hear a car or a motorcycle, or someone running. Nothing."

"A trying time for everyone involved," said Gus. "After the funeral, and the business with the will, what happened?"

"I went back to work," said Rachel. "It was important for me to continue to pay my way. Gerry earned enough that I didn't need to work, but I insisted. Sean was eighteen and was soon off to university. He spent his holidays here; of course, it was still his home. Byron left school that summer after failing most of his GCSEs. He knew where he wanted to be, and it wasn't at school doing A-Levels and going to university like Sean."

"He wanted to be on the green baize," said Gus.

"Exactly," said Rachel. "He was off to Q School. Gerry would have wanted me to help Byron achieve his dream, so I did everything I could. Sean wanted to follow in his father's footsteps."

"Who suggested employing a manager to cover the period between Gerry's death and Sean's graduating?" asked Luke.

"Nobody," said Rachel. "It was common sense. Daniel has been a godsend."

"That's Daniel Braund, is it?" asked Gus. "Where did you find him?"

"I advertised in the relevant magazines and interviewed the three people whose CV's appeared to match the same qualifications Gerry possessed. It's not rocket science. Daniel was the best candidate when I sat in the same room with the three people on my shortlist. I made the right choice. Daniel held the firm steady after it had lost its founder, made slight improvements in performance in the interim, and then helped Sean get settled. Daniel took the job believing it was for the short term. He's not far off retirement, but Sean valued his input so highly that he persuaded Daniel to stay."

"So, does Byron come home from time to time?" asked Gus.

"There's not much of an off-season with snooker," said Rachel. "The weather doesn't play a part. Byron's home for a week, here and there."

"What about Sean?"

"He sleeps here when he's not at his girlfriend's," said Rachel. "They met at university. She comes from Gloucester."

"Does his girlfriend come here?"

"Clare comes with Sean now and then."

"After Gerry died, was there ever an awkward moment with the boys?" asked Luke.

"You can't help yourself, can you? I loved Gerry. Yes, he was forty-nine when we met, and I was twenty-five. Gerry didn't bring me here to meet the boys at first. We met up for meals in restaurants in Bath and Trowbridge to break the ice. They knew their Dad was seeing someone. Then the four of us flew out to the Algarve and had a great holiday in the sun. Gerry told the boys in the car on the way back from Bristol Airport that I was coming to live with them."

"Did they accept you straight away?" asked Gus.

"There was never any animosity," said Rachel. "Of course, it took time for us to adjust. I'd never lived with anyone before. I was an only child, so I didn't have any experience of sharing a house with boys. I loved being around Gerry. Maybe I missed pointers that Sean and Byron resented me taking the place of their Mum, but they never said a word. It would be best if you asked them. As for awkward moments, Gerry and I slept at one end of the house, and the boys' bedrooms were far away. They used the family bathroom. Gerry and I had the en-suite. It was quite civilised, DS Sherman."

"I'm sure it was, Ms Cummins," said Luke. "But you can understand why Belinda Hogan took issue with a thirty-year-old single woman sharing a house with two teenage boys."

"Belinda accused me of corrupting a minor," said Rachel.

"Byron was sixteen when Gerry died," said Luke.

"I read the newspapers," said Rachel. "Teachers go to prison for having intercourse with a student, and teenage lads jump in bed with their mate's mother. Sean and Byron never tried it on with me. I wasn't interested in them. Gerry was everything to me. When he died, I didn't want to think about anyone else. Remember what I said earlier? Sean left home and went to university. Byron went to Q School. The only time the three of us have spent any length of time together under this roof was between the sixth of May and September when the boys started their new term or career. The three of us spent that time grieving for Gerry."

"Has there been anyone since for you?" asked Gus.

"I've had the same life as when I first moved to Bath, Mr Freeman. Trips to the theatre, concerts, the cinema, and evenings with friends I've met through work. I've visited restaurants with Daniel Braund and his wife. Daniel brought Simian along, a younger colleague from his previous firm in Bristol. We met several times after that, but there was no spark as far as I was concerned."

"You hinted that we could look around the house earlier," said Gus. "Is that possible?"

"I don't know how it will help find Gerry's killer," said Rachel.

She stood up, collected their cups, and put them on the tray.

"Follow me, and we'll start in the kitchen."

Gus and Luke trailed behind Rachel Cummins as she showed them each room on the ground floor. Luke gave a low whistle when they entered the gym.

"You could run classes at home with the professional equipment you have here."

"Never in a million years," laughed Rachel. "Gerry wanted this place to be a home, not an extension to the office,"

The games room was in good order, but the snooker table had a protective cover. A thin layer of dust on the rack holding cues and rests suggested it didn't get used as much as it did when the boys lived here full-time.

A good-sized lounge was at the front of the house with comfortable chairs and a wide-screen TV. A corridor between the lounge and games room walls led to the original building's right-hand extension. There Gus and Luke found a dining room and another small living room.

"We ate in the kitchen more often than not," said Rachel. "The extension was more Evelyn's domain. She and Gerry ate here, and Evelyn read in the smaller room or watched TV while Gerry and the boys watched sport."

"You have changed nothing at this end of the house?" asked Gus.

"I rarely come here," said Rachel. "Why would I?"

She led them upstairs to the large landing and pointed to the far end. Gus could see what she meant when she said the boys were far from the bedroom she and Gerry shared. The family bathroom was half the size of the entire floor area of his bungalow. The master en-suite was on the right-hand side of the corridor, next to one bedroom.

"That's Byron's room," said Rachel. "Sean's is opposite, next to Evelyn's studio."

"You haven't altered that either?" asked Gus.

"I've never set foot inside," said Rachel. "Gerry wanted it kept as it was when Evelyn flew to Sydney. Sean and Byron never asked for the key to open the door."

"Were you never tempted?" asked Luke.

"Never," said Rachel.

"I understand Gerry's reaction," said Gus. "My wife dropped dead from a brain aneurysm almost four years ago. I was in Swindon Crown Court, watching criminals face justice. They were men involved in a case I'd worked on before my retirement. After the guilty verdicts, my old team wanted to take me out to celebrate. I arrived home in a taxi late at night, thinking I'd creep in to bed next to Tess and apologise for getting drunk when I saw her in the morning. Instead, I found her on the kitchen floor with her hands covered in flour where she'd been baking. There was nothing anyone could have done. The doctor told me that Tess was dead before she hit the floor. Even if I'd been home that day, I couldn't have saved her. It took me a long time to come to terms with my loss. No doubt, it was the same for Gerry. I took Tess's newer clothes and accessories to charity shops and the other stuff to the tip. I've held on to several items that help keep her memory alive. Perhaps when Gerry was alone, he sat in that room, and Evelyn returned to him."

"He never said a thing to me," said Rachel.

"That's understandable, too," said Gus. "Gerry found you and, after five years, was ready to move on with a new relationship. However, there were two of you in that relationship, not three. Gerry would take care not to say Evelyn would do it this way or that Evelyn wanted that shrub to stay where it was. You avoid the east wing because that was Evelyn's domain. You didn't suggest converting the studio into your gym rather than extending the west wing to make the kitchen larger and house your gym on the ground floor."

"I take it you've had a similar experience?" asked Rachel.

"After Tess died, I spent months in our bungalow alone. We had just moved from Downton, near Salisbury, where we both worked for years. I didn't have friends to talk to, and I would have been miserable company if I had. I found my way out of the darkness in time, with the help of one villager and books Tess left lying around that I'd never had time to read. So when the opportunity arose to work with this team six months ago, I thought long and hard about whether it was what I needed. I took a chance, and not only was I working again, but I socialised. I found someone who had a similar effect on me as Gerry had on you. We've not lived together that long, but I've moved those few things of Tess's that I kept twice so far, and we've never sat down to talk about Tess in any detail. Her climbing roses on the bungalow wall are crying out for TLC, but Suzie wouldn't dream of suggesting she did something to them."

"That was how Gerry behaved," said Rachel. "What was in the past stayed in the past. I never felt able to raise the subject of Evelyn's lingering presence in the house. The layout of the rooms and the style of decoration all bear the stamp of a well-established, successful wildlife photographer. It was classy ten or fifteen years ago, but it's dated now. Gerry and the boys preferred to wrap themselves in Evelyn's creation. It helped keep her alive. Although Gerry loved me, and the boys accepted me, I could never make the place my own."

"Why didn't you sell up and move?" asked Luke. "It's too big. Sean and Byron will never come back here to live full-time."

Rachel looked at Gus.

"You can tell him."

"I haven't left my bungalow, have I, Luke? Even though Suzie has moved in, there's no question of us going anywhere, either. Ms Cummins has stayed here because the location suits her personal trainer career. Also, she feels a duty to Sean and Byron to keep the house until they decide to get their own homes. But, most of all, it's because every room she utilises in the house helps her keep Gerry's memory alive."

Luke nodded. Rachel Cummins gave Gus a brief smile.

"If we thought something in Evelyn's studio might explain Gerry's murder, would you let us have the key?" Luke asked.

"I'll fetch the key from the kitchen," said Rachel, "but I won't go in with you if you don't mind. It doesn't feel right."

Gus stayed on the landing while Luke and Rachel went downstairs.

Why did he need to unload his personal experiences on Rachel Cummins? In front of Luke as well? Was it this place? Gus shook himself. Just because the original building Gerry Hogan had transformed had stood for four centuries, it didn't mean it held magical properties.

Luke trotted upstairs with the key a minute later.

"It's okay, Luke, no rush," said Gus.

"That was for Rachel's benefit, guv. In case she asked again if I wanted to join one of her classes."

"Do you expect to find anything in here?"

"It would be daft not to look, guv."

Luke opened the door, and he and Gus stepped inside. Luke closed the door behind them.

The room was light and bright, with windows on two sides. Examples of Evelyn's work, certificates, and Gerry's wedding photographs covered the wall adjoining Sean's bedroom.

"It smells musty in here, guv," said Luke. "That confirms nobody has been here for the last six years."

"A shame," said Gus, "because it's a splendid room for a photographer or an artist. What else did Evelyn keep here, I wonder?"

Luke started opening drawers on filing cabinets. Gus sat at Evelyn's desk and rifled through letters and papers.

"No sign of a diary or letters that Evelyn kept from Gerry," said Gus.

"We've only got Rachel's word that Gerry didn't remove stuff from Evelyn's belongings before she appeared on the scene," said Luke. "If we found just one item to take with us for our meetings with Sean and Byron, it could help."

"What did she keep in the filing cabinets?" asked Gus.

"Correspondence with magazines and newspapers around the world, guv. Folders filled with photographs that Evelyn published over the years. She won or got nominated for many more awards than you would think by looking around the room. She hung her certificates on the wall, but not her awards. I wonder why?"

"Many people are modest about their accomplishments, Luke," said Gus. "The ones who make the most noise are usually those who have the most to be modest about."

"We didn't enter the main bedroom," said Luke. "I remember seeing photos downstairs of Gerry, Evelyn, and the boys when they were young. Perhaps an album covering the births and the boys as toddlers would be along the corridor?"

"Take a quick look, but be quiet, Luke. We're in danger of outstaying our welcome. Everything here is what I expected to find. If Evelyn had secrets hidden in a diary, she must have taken them to Australia. When the police recovered her personal items from the accident or her rented room, they might have dropped them off at her parents before Gerry flew out."

Luke padded along the corridor as quietly as possible and returned a few minutes later.

"I found several photo frames in a drawer that probably stood on the dressing table in the past, guv," said Luke. "There was a large album chronicling the first eighteen months to two years for each son."

"Is that normal?" asked Gus.

"I would say so, guv. I reckon typical behaviour is for parents to capture every new event in their child's life, and then year on year it becomes more of a chore, and later on, there are fewer landmarks to immortalise in living colour."

"Here's Luke with his first car, his first pint, and his first summons," said Gus. "Taken shortly after his seventeenth, eighteenth, and nineteenth birthdays. I didn't realise what joys I'd missed."

"Did you find a clue while I was gone, guv?"

"A letter from a wildlife conservation charity based in New South Wales offering Evelyn a senior position. The lure of the wild might have been greater than Gerry thought. He was happy for Evelyn to return to Australia for a month to carry out this commission at the Macquarie Pass National Park. Maybe she was planning on staying there for good."

"Would Nick Barrett be likely to have got wind of that?" asked Luke.

"Not sure," said Gus. "It's too late to get Neil to ask him this morning. We can ask the sons whether they knew their mother had itchy feet. They might have sensed the distance growing between their parents. They were only eight and six, so they were too young to spot such things."

"It's something new, guv," said Luke. "There's been no sign there was tension in the marriage. How could it relate to what happened in 2012?"

"I'm just checking the letter heading, Luke," said Gus. "The date of the job offer precedes the trip by three months. Maybe the National Park retrospective was Evelyn's way of getting the itch out of her system. I can't find a copy of a letter accepting or rejecting the job offer here."

"I'll make a note of the details, guv. Then, if the charity still functions, we can ask which way Evelyn Hogan jumped. How it could have any link to Gerry's murder, I can't fathom."

"We're swimming in treacle," said Gus. "Come on, let's get out of here. If we stay any longer, our host will wonder if we're angling for a lunch invite."

"Don't mention food, guv," said Luke. "I'm feeling peckish."

"I'll drive back via Bradford Road and find County Way, Luke."

"Gregg's, guv?"

"Our warm ovens are waiting for you, Luke. You know it makes sense."

"We can enjoy our hot snack on the drive back to the office, and Neil won't be any the wiser."

"He shouldn't be back yet, Luke. His meeting with Nick Barrett wasn't until eleven-thirty."

They walked downstairs. Luke tapped on the kitchen door to return the door key.

"Did you find anything useful?" asked Rachel.

"Too early to tell yet, Ms Cummins," said Gus.

"It was good to meet you, Mr Freeman," said Rachel, "I hope you finally find Gerry's killer."

"It won't be for lack of trying, Ms Cummins," said Gus.

Gus and Luke walked to the car.

"Will we need to come back, guv?" asked Luke.

"I can't think why except to tell Rachel we know who killed Gerry and why."

"Are we any closer to finding that person, guv?" asked Luke.

"I'm not even sure we're moving in the right direction, Luke. We could be getting further away. When you pop in to pick up our sausage rolls, grab a few napkins, could you, please?"

"Got it, guv. We don't want to return to the office with greasy fingers."

"I'm not worried about that, Luke," said Gus. "I don't want flaky pastry over the upholstery in the Focus."

Thirty minutes later, they were in the lift heading for the office. Blessing and Lydia looked up when the lift doors opened. Alex was nowhere in sight.

"Welcome back, guv," said Lydia. "Rewarding trip?"

"We picked up a few crumbs," said Luke.

"Where's Alex?" asked Gus.

"Restroom, guv," said Blessing. "It's his turn to make the coffee. We were breaking for lunch. Shall I ask him to fetch two more coffees?"

Gus nodded and sank into his chair. Luke was right; they had only got a few scraps of information this morning.

He wanted to take his time drinking this coffee and ponder its meaning.

Rachel Cummins didn't have twenty-twenty vision.

She might not have noticed if someone had parked a motorcycle near the gateway.

Was the motorcycle even relevant? The neighbour couldn't swear when he'd heard it pass his house. Although, he said it followed a sound like a backfire from a car or motorcycle.

What significance should they put on the lighting system in several of the rooms? Maybe the various additions to the house's floor area increased the chances that a doorbell or a phone ringing in the distant hallway could get missed.

What about the red light? Did that suggest Gerry Hogan had enemies? Or was he just taking sensible precautions to protect his family and their property? Thieves were more likely to attack a place that flaunted the trappings of wealth.

Another thing they learned was that Rachel used music in her training sessions. The amber warning light alerted her to the doorbell, but her headphones and the backing track would have masked the sound of the gunshot whenever it occurred.

She heard Sean call for his father when she was wrapping up her practice session and putting away her kit. Rachel had removed the headphones by a quarter to seven.

The letter to Evelyn Hogan from the charity had been in the house for three months. Did she show it to Gerry? Was he aware that Evelyn had received the job offer?

"A penny for them, guv," said Lydia.

"We've only spoken to two people so far," said Gus. "Nick Barrett and Rachel Cummins. Nick remembers Gerry Hogan as an honest, honourable family man with no enemies. Rachel loved him for five years and can't move on from an enormous house filled with memories of Gerry and his late wife, Evelyn. We can't shake their stories so far. The few vague anomalies from their interviews don't point me in any particular direction."

"Can I give you my take on this case, guv?" said Alex.

"Please do," said Gus.

"The murder file gives us details on what the investigation believed were the most significant events during Gerry Hogan's life. After school and university, he went to Australia with Nick Barrett. What made that trip significant?"

"Gerry met Evelyn, they fell in love, and she flew from the other side of the world to be with him," said Blessing. "How romantic that was. They got married soon after."

"What was his next significant life event?" asked Alex.

"Gerry set up his own business, they moved to Trowle Common, and started a family," said Lydia.

"So, they married in 1982, moved to Trowle Common in 1992," said Alex. "That's ten years with no apparent drama. The boys arrived in 1994 and 1996. Then, at the start of 2002, Evelyn gets killed on a business trip to New South Wales."

"We can discount Evelyn's death as a tragic accident," said Luke. "Another decade passed without signs that suggest Gerry had someone plucking up the courage to kill him," said Luke. "What are you driving at, Alex?"

"If Gerry's murder had occurred in the early Eighties, the trip to Australia would have made perfect sense as the catalyst for what happened. So how can it have impacted a murder that took place in 2012?"

"We've queried that more than once already," said Blessing.

"Move forward another ten years," said Alex. "The murder file didn't flag any event between 1982 and 1992 as significant enough to contact people to interview. What if Gerry had got killed during that time?"

"The police would have looked closer at the time Gerry spent working with Hargreaves Lansdown," said Gus. "I'll ask John Kirkpatrick whether they checked for client problems."

"The timing of the murder has to be significant, guv," said Alex. "The gap year trip and the period before Gerry Hogan became his own boss don't fit with May 2012. The only period left is between Evelyn's accident and the night of his death. Surely, the answer must lie there?"

"Are we missing a significant event in Gerry Hogan's life?" asked Lydia.

"He met Rachel Cummins, fell in love, and they lived together happily for five years," said Blessing. "I can't see how that could have been the catalyst for murder."

Chapter Seven

NEIL DAVIS HAD LEFT the Old Police Station office at five to eleven. When he reached Bradford-on-Avon, he hoped there would be a handful of vacant parking spaces in the station car park. He could still make Nick Barrett's office by half-past the hour.

Neil didn't expect a warm reception from the resident pit-bulls, Daphne and Suzanne, but at least they recognised him when he stepped inside the hallway and didn't keep him hanging around. They buzzed him straight through.

"Good morning, DS Davis," said Nick Barrett. "I've been considering what you asked for on the phone. I need to put on my thinking cap, don't I? You realise that asking a chap to cast his mind back thirty years to one particular night is a chore?"

"When you have eliminated the impossible, whatever remains, however improbable, must be the truth, sir," said Neil. "We need to check that none of the nights Gerry Hogan spent in someone else's bed didn't lead to his murder. Then, after we've done that, we can move on to another period in his life to search for what provoked the man's actions on the doorstep."

"I can see the logic behind that, DS Davis," said Nick Barrett. "If only it were elementary."

"Why not start from when you landed in Australia, sir," said Neil. "Or did Gerry Hogan join the Mile High Club on the flight from Singapore?"

"Gerry and I spent most of that journey sleeping," said Nick. "After we landed in Darwin, we stayed up as late as we could before crashing at our digs and didn't venture far until we got acclimatised."

"Jet lag?" asked Neil.

"Everybody reacts differently," said Nick. "We started setting our body clock to our destination time a day or two before we drove to Heathrow. We cut out the alcohol, drank plenty of water, ate in moderation, and slept between London and Singapore when we could. After the flight delay I mentioned, we were too tired to stick to the system. I was asleep before the safety checks."

"So, you spent the first few days in the city?"

"You won't remember Cyclone Tracy. It was before you were born," said Nick. "That cyclone flattened Darwin back in 1974. So, when we got there in 1981, they hadn't long finished rebuilding it. The city itself isn't much to write home about, but the nearby attractions more than compensate. One of our early trips was to a local cove, where we saw our first saltwater crocodiles. I can tell you that was an experience for two lads from Bradford-on-Avon. We travelled to and from the cove in a combi-van. I soon lost count of the number of trips we made in one of those. There were six of us altogether, plus our driver. Gerry and me, a guy from Cardiff and his girlfriend from our digs, plus two girls we collected from a hostel half a mile away."

"It didn't take long for Gerry to score after he recovered from jet lag, then?" said Neil.

"That was typical of Gerry. We spent the day at the cove, and when we made the return journey, he sat next to the prettiest girl of the pair. The other girl sat in the spare seat next to the driver. I knew it would not be my lucky day. Gerry persuaded the girls to join us for a drink in the Victoria Hotel. They had finished rebuilding that place four years earlier. The Vic was an institution in Darwin, one of its oldest watering-holes. The food was excellent too. We had showered, changed, and reached the bar at eight. The girls didn't make it until nine."

"The other girl was reluctant," said Neil. "I remember that experience. Can you remember their names or where they came from?"

"What I remember most was that they were on the last leg of their trip. Those two girls flew out of Darwin two days after we met. Although nothing happened for me during that brief encounter, it was great to meet them. They had been to Uluru, Alice Springs, the Great Barrier Reef, Sydney, and a couple more places we had on our wish list. I spent the evening asking Bronwen where the best hostels were and which tourist spots were worth visiting. Gerry and Cat left us to visit another well-known bar on Cavanaugh Street. We never saw them again before closing time. I walked Bronwen back to their hostel; she shook my hand and dashed inside. I was tipsy, staggered the half-mile to our digs, and fell asleep without getting undressed. Gerry was in the other bed when I woke up, but I had no clue what time he'd got in."

"Bronwen and Cat," said Neil, "where were they from? Can you remember?"

"Bronwen came from a seaside resort near Tenby," said

Nick. "Her accent was stronger than the couple from Cardiff. Bronwen didn't recognise them as Welsh, anyway. She termed them quasi-English and ignored them while we were at the cove. Bronwen's family spoke Welsh and went to chapel every Sunday. No wonder I only got a handshake."

Neil wasn't that interested in the Nick Barrett side of the story. He was interested in Gerry Hogan's companion that night.

"What about Bronwen's friend, Cat?" Neil asked. "Was she from the same part of Wales?"

"No, not a bit," said Nick. "Her accent was bland, not a regional one that you immediately recognise. Cat's voice wasn't posh, though, just neutral. Before I heard her speak, I guessed her name was Myfanwy, Megan, or another Welsh favourite. She wore a t-shirt with a kitten on the front and shorts."

"If they travelled together, surely Bronwen must have mentioned Cat's real name and where she lived?"

"I don't think they'd met before they got on the plane, DS Davis. Two young girls early twenties, on the adventure of a lifetime. Sensible enough not to risk travelling alone. We didn't see them after that night. We planned to move on, and they were getting ready for the long flight back to Blighty."

"Did Gerry say what happened that night?" asked Neil.

"I asked what time he got in. Gerry gave a big grin and went for a shower. I told your boss the other day Gerry didn't elaborate on any of his conquests."

"So he didn't know where his companion was going when she got home?" said Neil. "What jobs did these two have? Didn't you discuss that?"

"It wasn't the first thing on our list of things to talk about with girls we met, detective. Gerry and I had worked as a team for four or five years. Using underhand methods at university was impossible because most students knew you from somewhere. Also, it was open season in one of the city's nightclubs filled with locals."

"I don't think I follow you, sir," said Neil.

"The dating game has altered dramatically since those far-off days," said Nick. "Look, if it was a casual fling you were after in our day, you didn't give too much detail. For example, you might not use your real name or be vague about where you live. Or lie about what you did. Hi, I'm Gregg, a ski instructor from Windsor. That way, if things went pear-shaped, you didn't get a phone call a year later from a girl with a baby crying in the background."

"You're right," said Neil. "things have changed. So, who were you two that day?"

"Batman and Robin," said Nick. "Cassandra, the girl who met us at the airport, drove the combi-van to the cove. The girls laughed when they saw our t-shirts as they boarded the van. That broke the ice."

"So, you have no idea where either girl worked?"

"None whatsoever,"

"And you're certain neither Bronwen nor Cat mentioned where Cat lived?"

"I didn't speak to the girl much except at the cove. Cassie told us the best places to visit when the six of us were still in a group. I tried to make progress with Bronwen in the evening, but she wasn't interested. It was lucky that they had done so much travelling already. It would have made for a quiet night if they had arrived in Australia at the same time as us."

"I take it you didn't get in touch with Bronwen after you returned home?" asked Neil, "Or vice versa?"

"I don't think either of us believed there was any point, detective," said Nick.

"What about Gerry?"

"If he did, I didn't know," said Nick. "Gerry had met Evelyn by then. They were in love. He must have been because Gerry gave her his real name. But, no, Gerry had more sense than to chase up a one-night stand."

"Was that it for Darwin?" asked Neil.

"We stayed there for a further week. There were no more girls involved."

"Where did you go next?"

"Cassie introduced us to Mick, a fellow countryman who offered to give us a lift halfway to Alice Springs. He had various stops to make in outback towns on the way. That leg of the journey took us eight hours. We stayed in a grubby hotel overnight in a town that hardly needed a name because it was so small. There was a pub, so we drank a few lagers the next day. Cassie told us a truck would eventually come through on that route, and we could negotiate a lift. We stayed for five days in that dump. Then a trucker pulled in, and after another eight-hour slog, we reached Alice Springs."

"What was that like?" asked Neil.

"It's in the middle of nowhere," said Nick, "and only worth visiting if you want to visit Uluru, King's Canyon, and learn about the Flying Doctor."

"It did not impress you?"

"It must have been fifty degrees centigrade, detective. I was melting. Before you ask, no, Gerry didn't meet a girl in Alice Springs. We headed east after a week and made for Cairns. Our first stop was Mount Isa, four hundred miles away. We hired a car for that journey."

"I've never heard of the place," said Neil. "If there's just a mountain there, was it worth stopping?"

"Mount Isa is a city in the Gulf Country region of Queensland, DS Davis," said Nick Barrett. "It came into existence because of the vast mineral deposits in the area. The region has one of the most productive single mines in world history for lead, silver, copper, and zinc. Almost twenty thousand people lived there. We slept, refuelled, and made the six-hundred-mile trip to Cairns. That was where Gerry met Molly from Glasgow."

"Another pretty girl?" asked Neil.

"Molly was short, with a bubbly personality, and could drink both of us under the table," said Nick. "Gerry started up a conversation at Palm Cove. That was a thirty-minute bus ride from Cairns itself. There were hundreds of guys and girls there our age. They'd gathered for an impromptu barbie, and a guy with a guitar kept people entertained. Molly was with a party of five or six girls, but her mates wanted to go out on the town, not laze away the evening on the beach. So they jumped on the bus into town. I was on my Jack Jones, drinking bottled beer, grabbing a snack now and then, and minding my own business. I must have dropped off to sleep because Gerry and Molly had gone when I awoke. The barbie was cooling, and I had one bottle left."

"Did you miss the last bus?" asked Neil.

"Molly's pals caught that," said Nick. "I'd spent the night on the beach. No worries, as they say. The temperature only dropped to the low twenties centigrade. Warmer than an English summer's day."

"How did you get back to Cairns?" asked Neil.

"I caught the first bus of the morning. I must have reeked to high heaven. The few passengers on it gave me a wide berth. Gerry was sleeping when I reached the hostel. He had stamina; I'll give him that. We were drinking again at lunchtime and headed for Trinity Beach that night. He was off again."

"Molly caught up with him?"

"No, that night, it was Ruth and her friend, Shirley. Gerry went off with Ruth, and I got stuck with Shirley."

"I don't suppose you remember where they came from, surnames, or where they worked?" asked Neil, more in hope than expectation.

"Derby," said Nick. "both girls came from Derby and worked for Royal Crown Derby, the English porcelain manufacturer."

"Good, that's something we can follow up on," said Neil. "Is there anything to add to the Gerry and Ruth story? Was that another one-night stand?"

"You might see a pattern emerging, DS Davis," said Nick Barrett. "After a day spent imbibing the amber nectar, we visited our sixth or seventh bar, and Gerry saw Ruth. He told me to follow him and made a beeline for her. Ruth was taller than Molly and with a fuller figure. I prayed she had a twin sister somewhere in that crowded pub. Gerry bought our drinks and followed Ruth as she sashayed into a dark corner. I trailed along behind, as usual, to get introduced to Shirley."

"It didn't go well?" said Neil.

"She had the personality of a whelk, detective, and once she had another drink inside her, Shirley started to talk. A booming voice and language that would have caused my mother to faint. An hour later, when Gerry and Ruth disappeared to the girls' hostel, I could tell that Shirley expected to return to our digs with me. So I opted to walk along the Esplanade with her to give Gerry time alone with Ruth."

"How did Shirley react to that?" asked Neil

"I received a verbal onslaught rather than a physical one. For which I was grateful. Shirley would have made mincemeat out of me," said Nick. "She suggested I was gay. I went with her to the hostel to make sure she got back safely, made my excuses and left."

"What happened to Gerry?"

"He wasn't entirely happy when he returned. He thought he was in for an all-nighter."

"Were you sticking to Batman and Robin?" asked Neil.

"Gerry mislaid his t-shirt somewhere on the trip. I can't remember where. Somewhere between Alice Springs and Mount Isa. I think we were Gregg and Norm for that night."

"Did you move on from Cairns soon after?"

"We moved on to Port Douglas to visit the Great Barrier Reef," said Nick. "Now, that was an unforgettable experience. Amazing. Gerry and I had talked to one another again by then, but he wasn't keen on hitting on anyone. It was weeks before we left Queensland. We spent ten days in Mackay, just chilling out, trying to drink less and save our pennies. We knew the cost of living was higher around Sydney, and we wanted to keep money in reserve."

"Did you work during your trip?" asked Neil.

"I couldn't possibly comment, detective," said Nick. "One way of cutting back on the alcohol intake might be to pull a few pints for someone else. Let's leave it at that. We had a glorious time on the Sunshine Coast. The place became far more popular in the decade after we were there. It had attracted the hippies in the Sixties, people seeking an alternative lifestyle. There were craft industries, co-operatives, and spiritual centres wherever you looked. Far out, man. That stuff didn't interest us, but the weather was great, and the locals were friendly."

"When did Gerry's quiet period end?" asked Neil.

"After we moved into Brisbane," said Nick. "Now, let me see if I've got this right. I think her name was Julia, and she hailed from Richmond. The place on the Thames, not the town in Yorkshire. Julia did something in the City. She had a position with a merchant bank. Gerry was punching above his weight, but Julia took pity on him for four or five nights. She didn't have a friend in tow, so I didn't need to embarrass myself. I fell off the wagon, got drunk the first night, and had a hangover from hell, and that might have been an occasion when I pulled pints for other people. I kept my distance from Gerry and Julia in the evenings."

"Your hesitation suggests that Gerry got lucky more than once in Brisbane," said Neil.

"We're talking June, July, and the beginning of August," said Nick, leaning back in his chair and staring at the ceiling. "The weather was mild. There was no rush to move on, and it was the busiest time for tourism in the area. You couldn't go for a quiet pint anywhere. Every bar was teeming with international students. Their term dates differ from those in the UK. The academic year started in February and March, and they had a further intake in June and July. So, Brisbane was a paradise for Gerry when we stopped there. I couldn't drag him away. I was keen to move on to New South Wales and Sydney. Time was running out. We both wanted to fly home well before Christmas. He met a South African girl called Kerry, and I didn't see him again for a week. I'd resigned myself to my lot and didn't bother joining him when he was on the pull. I'd pick a bar, Brisbane had plenty to choose from, sit nursing a pint for two hours, then get off back to the digs."

"Time must have dragged," said Neil.

"Not really," said Nick, "I might have worked the odd shift, you know, and with so many students in town, I always had someone to chat to, male and female. So I kidded myself that it might happen when I least expected it if I didn't go looking for a girl."

"How did that work out for you?"

"Much as you might expect. Gerry was around during the day. We never fell out again. Oh, I've just remembered one more occasion before we left Brisbane. The weather was on the turn. They can get violent storms and cyclones there in August and September, so we agreed to heed the warnings and head south. We took one last excursion before leaving. We hired a car and drove north to Sylvan Beach, on Bribie Island."

"Was that a long trip?" asked Neil.

"Not compared to some we took. Only a ninety-minute drive. It was safe to swim in the cool blue sea. There were other tourists there, and when Gerry and I were walking back from our swim, he spotted two bronzed beauties sunbathing. He dropped down next to them and started talking. I joined them and got told to go forth and multiply. Gerry threw me the car keys and said he'd get a lift back somehow. I hung around for the rest of the afternoon, thinking he'd have a job separating them, but when dusk fell, I called it quits and drove back to Brisbane. Gerry persevered and ended up in bed with the pair of them."

"I thought you said Gerry didn't tell," said Neil.

"It was noon the next day before I saw him again. I was eating lunch at a café we used from time to time near our digs. I asked Gerry which girl had taken his fancy. He just winked and said, sometimes you didn't need to choose."

"Where were they from?" asked Neil.

"Romford in Essex," said Nick. "Their names were Mandy and Annette. Before you ask, they worked in a shoe shop. That was Gerry's last one-night stand. We moved to Sydney two weeks later. You know what happened there. Someone in a bar mentioned a beach party at Bondi the following evening, and we went along. Gerry spotted Evelyn strolling along the beach with her camera. That was the end of his philandering."

"You woke up next to a giant guy from New Zealand after another boozy night on the beach," said Neil.

"That was the one. When I saw Gerry later that day, I could tell that this latest girl had left a deeper impression than the others. It could have ended in tears, of course, but Evelyn felt the same way, and as soon as she was free to travel, she flew to the UK to join him in Bradford-on-Avon. I was the best man at their wedding. Evelyn didn't have bridesmaids, so I had no luck there either. It was the story of my life until I met Ginny."

"Are you sure there weren't any others?" asked Neil.

"Isn't that enough?" asked Nick.

Neil had to agree with him.

"We might be lucky in finding several of these women," said Neil, "especially the British ones. Whether any of them will lead us to Gerry's killer, who knows?"

"You can only do your best, DS Davis," said Nick Barrett.

Neil thanked the solicitor for his time and left the office. He still had thirty minutes left on the parking ticket he'd bought. Perhaps there was somewhere close by to grab a snack. Lunchtime would have come and gone before he reached the office.

Twenty-five minutes later, Neil arrived at the Old Police Station office and took the remaining space. Gus and Luke were back. Neil rode up in the lift to the first floor.

"Hi, guys," he said. "Miss me?"

"What did you learn, Neil?" asked Gus.

"I reckon Gerry Hogan was lucky to last as long as he did, guv," said Neil. "He was a lad and no mistake."

"How many names did you get?" asked Blessing.

"Surnames and addresses would be more helpful," said Lydia.

"I can't help you there, ladies," said Neil. "The best Nick Barrett could come up with was eight first names and a nickname. I got a few hometowns and occupations, but that was it."

"Nine girls?" asked Blessing.

"Gerry only slept with seven of them," said Neil. "Bronwen from Tenby talked to Nick Barrett for hours about places she'd visited in Australia over the previous weeks. Shirley from Derby got escorted back to her hostel by Nick. She was keen, and he wasn't."

"Enter everything into the files, Neil," said Gus. "Luke and I have added what we learned this morning from Rachel Cummins. You can catch up on that later. Luke, why don't you call Nick Barrett now? Catch him before he disappears for a long lunch."

"Did I forget something, guv?" asked Neil.

"I found a letter offering Evelyn a job in New South Wales," said Gus. "There was no sign that she'd accepted or turned it down. Unfortunately, we can't ask Gerry whether he knew about the offer. Perhaps Nick can tell us if Gerry had passed the information on to him."

"Over a frame of snooker at the club?" said Neil. "Yes, that's a possibility. One thing I picked up while Nick was chuntering on about his lack of female company. When he

121

rebuffed Shirley's ample charms, she returned to her digs and disturbed Gerry and Ruth, Gerry was miffed, and he and Nick hardly spoke for a day or so. Other than that, they remained good buddies throughout the nine months they were out there."

"Nick Barrett has confirmed that he knew nothing of a job offer, guv," said Luke a few minutes later. "He was surprised to learn there had been one. Nick thought Evelyn was happy here in the UK."

"Fine. Thanks, Luke. When can you call that charity to find out what happened?"

"It's early Thursday morning there now, guv," said Luke.

"Look it up on the internet, Luke," said Gus. "Find a contact email address. Send the request for information, and maybe we'll get a response soon after they open their offices for the day. It could be informative, but it's not urgent."

"Got it, guv."

Gus checked the murder file for details on John Kirkpatrick. He found a mobile number for DCI Kirkpatrick with Avon & Somerset Police in Portishead and called him.

"Is that John Kirkpatrick? Good afternoon, sir. Gus Freeman here, former DI in Salisbury. I work with a Crime Review Team for ACC Kenneth Truelove from London Road. I'm sure you remember him. Can I pick your brains on a murder case we're re-investigating?"

"I hope it won't take long, Gus. I'm on TV this evening, and the crew is setting up outside the building. You've got two minutes."

"Gerry Hogan, sir. Shot on his doorstep on the sixth of May six years ago on Trowle Common. We can't find anything between 1982 and 1992 when he worked for Hargreaves Lansdown. Was every one of his business dealings without blemish? Didn't you find even one of his clients worth an interview?"

"I remember that case, Gus. It isn't the only one I've had to leave unfinished, but everything we tried led to a dead end. Vicky Bennison was my number two back then. She trawled through the various clients that Hogan handled. The guy was as honest as the day was long as far as Vicky could assess. She was an excellent officer. If there was something dodgy, and Vicky didn't find it, then I was happy to move on to hunt for the killer elsewhere."

"Many thanks, sir," said Gus. "You probably need to dash to make-up. I'll update you if we find a new lead. We've made little progress so far."

"Bye, Gus. I wish you luck."

Gus sat back in his chair and puffed out his cheeks.

"Another dead end, guv?" asked Alex.

"Kirkpatrick doesn't think Gerry Hogan did anything in the Eighties to warrant getting shot. They dug into the clients that Hogan handled for Hargreaves Lansdown, and he came up smelling of roses."

"When everyone gets the chance to read through my notes on this morning's meeting, I think we'll agree that Nick Barrett revealed more about the nature of the relationship between him and Gerry Hogan."

"That was a long speech for you, Neil," said Luke.

"Cheeky. I meant that from the details in the original murder file, we thought of Gerry Hogan as honest and honourable, a faithful husband and father. A man with no enemies. Nobody could believe that anyone could want him dead."

"If Hogan slept with seven women on that Australian

trip," said Blessing Umeh. "How many others had he bedded while at university?"

"Barrett described a routine the pair followed when they were in a bar or nightclub," said Neil. "Somewhere they hadn't visited before, where none of the girls knew who they were."

"We've both met Nick Barrett, Neil," said Gus. "I didn't peg him as a serial womaniser. Even if he benefitted from hanging onto the coattails of a man who was irresistible to women."

"You're more inclined to believe the Australian trip was just Gerry Hogan sowing his wild oats, guv," said Lydia. "One last fling before knuckling down to working life. If he hadn't met Evelyn, who had such a profound effect on him, Hogan would probably have returned home, met a local girl in the next couple of years, married, and settled down."

"That's the impression I formed of the man," said Gus. "Nobody in the original investigation, nor any of us, has found a thing to suggest Gerry was ever unfaithful to Evelyn. Belinda would have known or made it her business to find out, especially when looking for ways to challenge the will. No, I believe Hogan acted in the manner that Neil described. It's not unheard of for students to experience a sexual awakening as part of their time at college or university, and I've lost count of media reports about Brits abroad enjoying a hedonistic lifestyle the minute they get the Mediterranean sun on their backs. It takes two to tango. Gerry Hogan found willing partners both at home and abroad. Nick Barrett wasn't as fortunate. That's life."

"Do we continue to look at the names Neil brought back, guv?" asked Blessing. "Or are you saying they're a waste of time?"

"I'm drawing a dotted line under the bed-hopping that

occurred between Hogan leaving school and getting married," said Gus. "We can't rule out a connection to his death until you've received information from the Hub that removes any lingering doubts. As soon as you can do that, we'll draw a solid line under it and move on, No, we continue to probe for a connection."

"The mystery remains then, guv," said Neil. "If the killer didn't come from the period between 1976 and 1992, then they must have had a serious disagreement with Hogan between them moving to Trowle Common and the months before his death."

"That puts the focus firmly on the work I've been carrying out," said Alex.

"If it were easy to spot in the company accounts, you would have found it by now," said Gus.

"Hogan made piles of money from his business, guv," said Luke. "That suggests he was an expert. It also means that if he wanted to bury his mismanagement of funds, he could bury the evidence so deep that we would struggle to find it. We aren't financial experts."

"Good point, Luke," said Gus. "No offence, Alex, but we'll hand the task over to the forensic accountants in the Hub."

"Fair enough, guv," said Alex. "It felt like a hopeless task from the start. I haven't spoken with Daniel Braund yet, but the business continues to thrive, and he's experienced enough to know whether the firm he was employed to oversee was built on firm foundations or shifting sands. Unless he's a crook, too, then you would hope he would report any issues back to Rachel Cummins. The Hub will return to us quickly, confirming everything was above board."

"We're back to Gerry Hogan, the individual who was as honest as the day is long," said Gus.

"I'll try to find something to dirty his reputation tonight, guv," said Neil.

"When do we speak to Sean Hogan, Luke?" asked Gus.

"Tomorrow afternoon, guv. Two o'clock."

"Have you got anyone fixed for the morning?"

"Who did you have in mind, guv?"

"Belinda Hogan," said Gus.

"I'll get in touch with her, guv. I've emailed the charity and received a generic acknowledgement of receipt."

"We can't get on top of this case despite doing the right things, guv," said Neil.

"I'm glad you think we're on the right track, Neil," said Gus. "I've been sitting here wondering where on earth to look next. I'm baffled."

The team spent the rest of the afternoon on their given tasks while Gus checked the Freeman Files. Had they taken a wrong turning somewhere? Had someone they'd interviewed lied to them or kept back vital evidence?

Gus sat alone in the office when everyone had left for the day.

He often found that this was when a light shone in the darkness. While the room buzzed with activity, it could distract him. After five minutes of trying to find inspiration, Gus decided it was time to drive home. He knew what the problem was now. This case had started with a handful of family members and friends that Kirkpatrick and Bennison interviewed.

After a few days of asking Nick Barrett and Rachel Cummins different questions to those posed six years ago, there were now too many characters.

Chapter Eight

GUS ARRIVED home at a quarter to six and spotted Suzie's Golf in its usual spot. He hoped she was feeling as cheerful as she had this morning.

"I'm home," he called as he walked into the hallway.

"Dinner will be ready in five minutes," said Suzie. "I thought you were never coming home."

"We're getting nowhere on the Hogan case," said Gus. "When Neil spoke to Nick Barrett today, he got too many leads for us to investigate. So I'm not sure it was useful. There's too much crowding into my thoughts."

"You can't see the wood for the trees," said Suzie. "What's on your list for tomorrow?"

"I'm seeing the victim's sister in the morning and his eldest son in the afternoon. Neil's off to a snooker club this evening. There's an outside chance he'll find dirt on our victim that his partner, Rachel, and best friend, Nick Barrett, have hidden from us."

"How did the meeting with Rachel go this morning?" asked Suzie.

"I found her easier to talk to than I imagined," said Gus. "She's a smart cookie, that one. There was one odd thing. Gerry kept his late wife's photographic studio locked. He refused to change a thing; Rachel had never been in the room. We asked to take a look, and she was happy to give us the key. We found little except a letter containing a job offer in New South Wales for Evelyn."

"Was Evelyn leaving Gerry?" asked Suzie.

"Nick Barrett didn't believe so. He thought their marriage was rock solid."

"Maybe, tonight and tomorrow will bring you more luck," said Suzie.

"By the close of play tomorrow, I hope to define the strategy we need to follow over the coming days. So far, we've added more variables into the mix."

"Let's get stuck into our cheese omelette and chips," said Suzie. "I've looked forward to this. You must be hungry, too?"

"You bet," said Gus. He decided to forget the large sausage roll that he and Luke had devoured at lunchtime.

Later that evening, they wandered along the lane towards the Lamb.

"I'd like to check on my allotment before we go inside," said Gus. "I appreciate things have fallen behind. At least I'll have a better idea of the scale of the problem on Saturday afternoon."

Suzie stood beside Gus's garden shed while he wandered the length of the plot and back.

"It's as if I've been on holiday for a fortnight," he said. "I can remember Bert's words to me this time last year. Everything comes into season at once and needs picking in August. So don't take time off without getting another gardener to keep an eye on things."

"Bert's had plenty on his mind," said Suzie, "with Irene in hospital. He hasn't had time to look after your plot and his own."

"It's unreasonable of me to expect him to bother," said Gus. "He's well into his eighties. He offered to help when I returned to work, but the time has come for me to do my bit."

Bert Penman was the only familiar face they spotted as they entered the bar.

"Evening, Mr Freeman, Miss Ferris," said Bert.

"We've just dropped by the allotments, Bert," said Gus.

"I thought you'd forgotten where they were," said Bert with a grin.

"I'll be back in harness on Saturday afternoon, Bert," said Gus. "I've relied on you for too long. Anyway, how are you? And how's Irene now? Is she home?"

"Irene discharged herself this afternoon, Mr Freeman," said Bert. "Her stomach was only grumbling now and again. She thought she'd be able to recover better at home. I'm keeping her stocked with vegetables from my patch. The Reverend is monitoring her liquid intake, if you get my drift. There will be no more unsupervised manufacture of cocktails."

"Did they ever decide which ingredient caused the problem?" asked Suzie.

"It wasn't one thing in particular, Miss," said Bert. "Irene seems to have developed intolerances that have sprung up in the last few years. She's eaten fruit for seventy years with no side effects. Now the Reverend tells me the fructose in the watermelons, grapes, and apples she added to her most recent cocktail played havoc with her digestion."

"These things are sent to try us, Bert," said Gus.

"It never used to happen though, Mr Freeman," said Bert, taking a good swig of his pint of cider. "The Reverend told me she happily got through the hay fever season as a child. She thought she'd picked up a chill when she started sneezing earlier this year. Instead, one of her parishioners told her it was hay fever. Now, why should that start up at her time of life? I reckon it's something in the water, Mr Freeman. That's why I'm sticking to cider."

"You'd better pray you don't develop a fructose intolerance, Bert," said Gus.

"Is the Reverend with Irene this evening?" asked Suzie.

"Brett collected her from the rectory after he dropped me here," said Bert, "I'm expecting to see them after they've got Irene settled."

"Did you go to see her last night?" asked Suzie.

Bert gave Suzie an old-fashioned look.

"Brett and the Reverend didn't give me much choice," said Bert. "They whisked me out of my house and into the car before I had time to catch my breath."

"I'm glad you went, Bert," said Suzie. "Irene would have been disappointed if you hadn't made an effort. You two have grown close over these past months."

"We're not as close as you two, Miss Ferris," said Bert. "Don't rush out to buy a hat. Mrs North and I are good companions. That's as far as we want things to go."

"Are you ready for another pint, Bert?" asked Gus. "I'm in the chair. We've stood here for several minutes without troubling the landlord."

"I don't like to go thirsty, Mr Freeman," said Bert. "What will you be drinking tonight, Miss Ferris, another one of those fancy soft drinks you've taken a liking to?"

"You don't miss much, Bert Penman," said Suzie. "They're a refreshing drink in the summer."

"Whatever you say, Miss," said Bert, giving Suzie a wink.

Gus handed Bert a fresh pint, and he and Suzie wandered outside to watch the sun disappear over the distant hills.

"I'm sure Bert knows," said Suzie.

"I haven't breathed a word," said Gus. "Who could have let it slip?"

"Nobody," said Suzie. "Do I look different to you?"

"Not at all," said Gus. "You're blooming."

"That doesn't help, Gus Freeman," said Suzie.

"I think we'll call it a night after this one," said Gus. "It's been a long day, and I've got another gruelling day ahead tomorrow. We'll catch up with the gang at the weekend."

"Okay, we'll ask Bert to say hello to Brett and the Reverend and tell him we've got a bottle of eighteen-year-old Macallan's at home that's calling our name."

"I like the sound of that," said Gus.

"The sound is all you're going to get, Gus," said Suzie. "I've hidden it to bring out for an appropriate celebration."

"It's VJ-Day today," said Gus. "I read it somewhere. Does that qualify as appropriate?"

"I meant an appropriate personal celebration," said Suzie. "Our special occasion."

Seven months and counting, thought Gus.

NEIL DAVIS PARKED in the railway station car park yet again. He'd only visited the town on a couple of occasions before this week, and tonight was his third trip since Tuesday. He soon found the club on Market Street. The place looked quiet—no big surprise. The professionals might play throughout the year, but Neil knew local leagues were most active between September and April. Neither of the two tables was in use a few minutes after eight. Two men stood at the bar, chatting with the barman. All three looked to be in their fifties or sixties. Sean Hogan wasn't in tonight. Neil knew he could stay for a while and hoped to learn something useful.

Thursday, 16 August 2018

GUS AND SUZIE left the house at eight-thirty on the dot.

"Your turn to cook tonight," she said after she kissed him and walked to the Golf.

"A quiet night in with our feet up," said Gus. "To prepare for a late-night on Friday night."

"I'll see you tonight," said Suzie. "Good luck today."

"We'll need it," said Gus, getting behind the wheel of his Focus.

Suzie led the way into Devizes, and Gus remembered that Blessing was heading to London Road this morning. She delivered the information Neil had gathered from Nick Barrett, plus the financial statements that Alex had started to untangle. Gus wanted to visit the Hub to get things moving, but he knew Neil needed to divulge what he learned last night before their appointment with Belinda Hogan.

He and Suzie exchanged their usual waves, and Gus drove past London Road, past the brewery and out of Devizes, heading for the Old Police Station office.

When he arrived, he saw three spaces lying empty. He parked and went upstairs in the lift.

"Morning, guv," said Lydia.

"Ah, you and Alex came together this morning," Gus said.

"There's no fooling you, guv," said Neil.

"Can you justify this claim for expenses I can see on my desk, DS Davis?"

"I only had a pint and a half of bitter, guv. An hour on the snooker table and petrol for fifteen miles there and back. I grabbed a bag of chips on the way to the car."

"Was it worth going?" asked Gus.

"Neither Neil Barrett nor Sean Hogan came into the club last night, guv. The steward explained that I could fill in a form and get a provisional membership for two months. I mentioned Nick Barrett's name when he asked if I knew a club member. That didn't automatically get me a permanent membership, and it didn't exclude me, either. Make of that what you will. My application has to go before the committee for final approval."

"Never mind, Neil," said Gus. "You were unlikely to go back there."

"You could be right, guv," said Neil. "Anyway, as soon as I'd filled out the form, I could use all the facilities. So I played snooker with one of the old guys that had been at the bar. His mate had gone home."

"Not rushed off their feet in there, then?"

"Middle of August, guv," said Neil. "The steward said it picks up after the Bank Holiday weekend."

"Any breaks?" asked Alex.

"Twenty-two in the second frame," said Neil.

"In the case, I meant," said Alex.

"I walked right into that one, didn't I?" said Neil.

"Well?" asked Lydia.

"The old guy, Jimmy, he remembered Gerry Hogan. They were at school together. Guess what he said?"

"Honest as the day is long. Didn't have an enemy in the world," said Gus.

"Jimmy told me that Gerry Hogan was the quiet, studious type. Not the typical teenager he associated with in the town. The original murder file painted Gerry as someone who avoided trouble. While Jimmy and his pals visited Trowbridge or one of the other local towns looking for trouble on a Saturday night, Gerry would come to the snooker club. Jimmy said he remembered when Nick Barrett and Gerry started going around together."

"After Nick's twelfth birthday," said Gus.

"That was typical of Gerry," said Neil, "according to my snooker opponent. Nobody in Jimmy's crowd had the time of day for Nick Barrett. He was a chubby lad who didn't enjoy the rough and tumble of their sports at school. Nick was always an outsider. Gerry excelled at most sports but refused to get drawn into his colleagues' social lives, even though he played for the school teams. Once the matches had ended, he showered, changed, and went home. Nick invited Gerry to his posh birthday parties. That was it, apart from a couple of Nick's cousins and another loser from the same year at school. The Barrett family had loads of money, and the parties were far grander than the average Bradford kid enjoyed. Jimmy reckoned Gerry needed someone to tag along with who would always be well-behaved. Someone with a bland personality who would help Gerry stay on track for the career he planned. He invited Nick to his birthday parties, plus a handful of his sporting friends. Jimmy never got an invitation. The quieter, more intellectual type who was good at football or cricket got the invites."

"That ties in with everything we learned from the murder file," said Alex.

"It's as if Gerry didn't trust himself not to get into trouble, guv," said Lydia. "Did he have a short fuse? What about his father? Was there any history there?"

"Gerry's parents are both dead," said Gus. "We can't ask them. I can ask Belinda when I speak to her later. Would it be possible for a boy of twelve to understand his potential for violence, Lydia?"

"Violence is a learned behaviour, guv, according to experts. There's a strong association between exposure to violence and the use of violence by young adolescents. Whether a twelve-year-old Gerry Hogan was aware of a violent gene passed on to him by his father and attempted to control matters is a stretch. He would have encountered pressure situations in those school matches that caused him to lash out or have a temper tantrum. There's been no mention of that. Quite the opposite. Unless Nick Barrett and Rachel Cummins lied, Gerry was an even-tempered, friendly guy."

"It won't hurt to ask," said Gus. "Neil, did Jimmy offer any instances where Gerry Hogan's association with Barrett caused a rift with other students? If Jimmy and his mates got into scraps with teenagers from local towns, what about Bradford-on-Avon? Did a few tearaways pick a fight with Gerry and Nick as they left the snooker club, for example?"

"Nothing, guv. Jimmy and his mates played snooker and pool in the club occasionally. Gerry and Nick kept to themselves. The club didn't stand for any troublemaking. Things ended when Gerry and Nick left school and went to university."

"Jimmy left school and found a job, did he?" asked Gus.

"He went to college in Trowbridge for two years, guv,"

said Neil. "Then he worked at a local rubber factory throughout his working life. He retired as a Technical Manager."

"Did he see much of Gerry when he returned from Clifton to live at Trowle Common?" asked Gus.

"Like most husbands and fathers, guv, Jimmy didn't use the club much in his twenties and thirties," said Neil. "When his kids were older, he started dropping in once a week for a few pints and a frame of snooker with a colleague. Jimmy saw Gerry and Nick there often in the early Nineties. He told me they hadn't changed. Gerry was still quiet, polite, and friendly towards the other members. Nick Barrett was the same pompous oaf he'd been at school. Jimmy couldn't understand why they continued to spend time together. Gerry was more successful than the solicitor who inherited the family firm."

"Perhaps Gerry Hogan wanted something different from the high-powered financial life he had to cope with daily," said Luke. "The club, and Nick Barrett, kept him grounded. Don't forget Gerry took his sons there too as soon as they were old enough."

"What did Jimmy make of Sean and Byron?" asked Gus.

"Sean is a chip off the old block," said Neil. "A one-track mind, the same as his father. He went into the Hogan firm straight from university. Sean didn't barge in and try to take over. Jimmy said Sean had the sense to let Daniel Braund ease him in gradually and hand over the reins when the time was right. Sean has always had an eye for the ladies, like his father. There were no dramas with any of the girls he went out with while he was at school, Jimmy didn't know about the university years, but Clare, the current girlfriend, has been with Sean for years. Sean didn't follow his father's example and take a gap year."

"That's understandable," said Alex. "He was sitting his A-Levels when his father died and then went to university in September. Three years ago, when he returned to the firm with his degree, he could already have started seeing Clare. Not so easy to take a year out without taking her with him."

"What did Jimmy have to say about Byron?" asked Gus.

"He's brilliant, guv," said Neil, "There's an honours board on the wall next to the main match table. His name has been featured there every year since 2010. He recorded over thirty century breaks before he left to start his professional career. There were no maximum breaks on those tables, but he's had three on tour since he left home to travel the world. They love Byron at the club. He's far more outgoing than Sean or his late father."

"Byron is more like his late mother, Evelyn, isn't he?" asked Lydia.

"That's what Nick Barrett told us," said Gus. "Less academically gifted than Sean, but just as focussed on the path that he followed."

"When Jimmy and I finished our two frames of snooker, he went home, guv," said Neil. "I tried to get another opinion from the steward, but he wasn't there when Gerry was alive. He told me he had moved to Bradford-on-Avon from Bridport, in Dorset, four years ago. He knew Sean and Byron were club members but hadn't seen enough of them to comment."

"Jimmy must have known Nick Barrett, surely?" asked Gus.

"Barrett is on the committee, guv," said Neil. "If I read the steward right, Nick Barrett wouldn't win a popularity contest in the club if he was the only entrant."

"Well, it was a night out, Neil," said Alex. "A pity it wasn't more productive."

"Time will tell," said Gus. "Talking of time. When am I due at Belinda Hogan's place, Luke?"

"Half-past ten, guv," said Luke. "She still lives in the family home. I'll give you the address before you leave."

Gus heard the lift descend to the ground floor. Blessing was back.

"Anything from that charity yet, Luke," asked Gus.

"Nothing yet, guv."

Blessing Umeh exited the lift and walked to her desk.

"Both jobs are on the Hub's schedule for today, guv," she said. "Divya hopes to have interrogated the various social media sites by tonight for connections between the names Neil supplied. The forensic accountant I spoke to will apply various skills and methods to determine whether there has been financial reporting misconduct at Hogan's."

"Well done, Blessing," said Gus. "After you've updated your digital files, you can catch up with Neil's night out. He should have got everything done by then."

"Got it, guv," said Blessing.

Gus got up and headed for the restroom.

"Are you okay, Blessing?" asked Lydia.

"I suppose so," said Blessing. "You know how Wednesday evenings are for me. My mother calls me and expects to get a detailed account of everything we've done at work. She asked if I'd met anyone new since Dave finished with me. I mentioned we were going out on Friday night, and she asked who was going. Were they the right people? You know what I mean. I'm twenty-one, but some-times my parents treat me like I was twelve."

"I can vaguely remember those days," said Lydia. "My foster parents weren't too strict, thank goodness. They gave me a degree of leeway. If I stayed out later than they said or spent time with people they didn't know, it could mean my free time got cut. The more I played by their rules, the better things became. It was an easy decision."

"My father must have listened in because when I said I was going with Divya, I could hear him tutting in the background."

"Did you speak to him?" asked Lydia.

"Not last night," said Blessing. "My mother asked whether I was visiting them this weekend. I said I would drive over on Sunday afternoon. She was disappointed that I wasn't going earlier, so I could attend church with them."

"Did you regularly go when you lived near Warwick?" asked Lydia.

"My parents never gave me a choice," said Blessing. "At least, until I became a police officer. Then I could volunteer to work the occasional Sunday. I stopped going when I moved to Worton with Mr and Mrs Ferris. Nobody stood at the bottom of the stairs asking if I'd dressed in my Sunday best clothes yet."

"Has your father tested out the journey into Bath from Englishcombe yet?" asked Alex.

"I'll find out on Sunday," said Blessing. "He has six weeks before his students arrive to start the new year. Four miles is no distance, but my father's sense of direction is so poor that my mother fears for him every day he leaves the house. Perhaps I should go with him after dinner to show him the way."

"Are you sure you know how to get there, Blessing?" asked Lydia.

"It's the only thing I have to remind me of Dave. He wrote out the route for me and put it in my glove box for safe-keeping."

"You might be late on Monday morning then," said Alex.

"Don't get on at her, Alex," said Lydia. "Blessing is nervous enough as it is."

Gus was back at his desk with a coffee. Blessing noticed that Neil had a fresh cup too.

"Is Neil going with you this morning then, guv?" she asked.

"I hadn't given it much thought, Blessing. I thought Alex would be best to take with me to talk to Sean Hogan this afternoon. Why? D'you fancy a trip to Bradford-on-Avon?"

"Yes, please, guv. I've never been there."

"Okay then," said Gus, looking at the clock on the far wall. "If you want a coffee before we go, you'd better get cracking."

As Blessing walked to the restroom, Luke approached Gus's desk.

"Here's Belinda Hogan's address in Barton Orchard, guv. I've had a reply from the charity. There's been quite a turnover in personnel since 2002. The HR manager had found the relevant file and could confirm that Evelyn rejected the job offer. Their Chief Financial Officer was the only senior member of staff still on site from those days. The HR manager said he'd asked her what she remembered. The CFO told him that Evelyn wanted to use the National Park commission as a stepping-stone to returning to Australia with her family. Evelyn wanted the boys to love Australia as much as she did, and when the two of them spoke over the phone, Evelyn said that Gerry's business was changing all the time. More and more of the business took place online. Evelyn couldn't see why Gerry couldn't operate just as easily in New South Wales as he did in West Wiltshire."

"Thanks, Luke," said Gus. "As one door closes, another one slams in your face."

"We're running out of loose ends, guv," said Luke.

Fifteen minutes later, Blessing and Gus were in the lift and heading for the car park.

"Nissan Micra, or Ford Focus, guv," said Blessing.

"I know where we're going, Blessing," said Gus. "It's not that I don't trust your driving."

"If you say so, guv,"

Gus drove them into Bradford-on-Avon and found a parking space after a five-minute wait.

"Busy here today, guv," said Blessing.

"We're due at Ms Hogan's house in around ten minutes," said Gus. "We'll walk, as it's such a pleasant morning. This car park is always busy. We've hit a changeover period for mothers and toddlers, and the public at the indoor swimming pool over there."

"It's a town with a long history, by the looks of it. This bridge over the river, for a start."

"Built by the Normans," said Gus. "Although they were here long after the Romans."

"I don't suppose that's a surprise, guv. Bath is only a few miles away."

"How do you think this case is going, Blessing?" asked Gus.

Blessing stopped on the bridge and looked into the River Avon below.

"Rather like that duck, guv," said Blessing. "Drifting."

Chapter Nine

GUS QUICKENED HIS STEP. Five minutes later, they reached Barton Orchard.

"Very nice," said Blessing. "What d'you reckon, guv, three-quarters of a million?"

"Quite likely," said Gus. He rang the doorbell.

Belinda Hogan answered and invited them into a small anteroom off the hallway.

Belinda was now sixty-three years old, two years older than Gus. He'd seen photographs of Gerry and understood why he had been so successful with women. It was plain that the woman who sat opposite him this morning was Gerry's sister, yet there was a certain sadness in her eyes and a pinched look around her mouth that was unattractive. Perhaps Rachel Cummins was right.

"What progress have you made?" demanded Belinda.

"Don't you want to see our credentials first?" asked Blessing. "When we've established who we are and why we're here, then Mr Freeman will ask the questions. That's the way these things work. I'm sorry if you were mistaken."

Gus waited for the reaction. He didn't know what to expect from Blessing. She was as quiet as a mouse most of the time, and then without warning, she exploded.

Belinda's lips moved, but no sound came out.

"I'm DC Blessing Umeh," said Blessing, "and here's my warrant card. My boss is Mr Freeman, a consultant with Wiltshire Police. We're reviewing your brother's murder case from May 2012. This week we have spoken with Mr Barrett, a solicitor friend of your brother, and Ms Rachel Cummins, Gerry's partner at the time of his death. I should advise you that Mr Freeman is interviewing your nephew, Sean Hogan, at two o'clock this afternoon."

"I wish you had come to me first," said Belinda. "Nick Barrett is a fool, and that Cummins woman knows more about Gerry's death than she's admitting."

Blessing sighed. Gus thought she was going to give Belinda Hogan both barrels. Time to intervene.

"Good morning, Ms Hogan. Perhaps we can start again. Our task is to discover the identity of your brother's killer. The way I intend to do that is to ask those who knew the victim best what they remember of him. Something they tell me will explain why Gerry became a target. Everyone we've interviewed has repeated the same things they told DI Kirkpatrick and DS Bennison in 2012. Gerry was honest, hardworking, a good father, a faithful husband, and a keen sportsperson. Gerry didn't have an enemy in the world. I don't believe that's a person who gets shot in the head on his doorstep, do you? So if Gerry was the complete opposite of those things, yes, it's understandable that he'd attract the attention of someone who thought the world would be a better place if Gerry Hogan left it."

"Gerry *was* all of those things," said Belinda. "A good man."

It was the first time Gus had seen any sign of genuine emotion.

"You described Nick Barrett as a fool," said Gus. "What do you mean by that?"

"Nick trailed behind my brother like a faithful puppy," said Belinda. "It was pathetic when Gerry was in his early teens. It was far worse when they were at university and afterwards."

"Did you see much of them when they studied in Bristol?" asked Gus.,

"They didn't live on campus," said Belinda. "Gerry stayed here most of the time, and Nick lived at their home out at Turleigh."

"That's close to the town, is it?" asked Gus.

"Two miles from this house, out towards Winsley," said Belinda. "They both had cars and took turns driving into Bristol."

"What were you doing?" asked Blessing. "You were three years older than Gerry and Nick. Have you been to university?"

"My parents needed me here at home," said Belinda, staring into her lap. Her hands twisted the handkerchief she held. Blessing felt sorry for the wretched piece of blue cloth that matched the colour of the woman's blouse.

Gus could tell that was when the light had faded in this woman's life.

"Did you and Gerry arrive late in your parents' life?" he asked.

"My mother, Jean, was forty-one when I came along. She and my father, Peter, had almost given up hope of having a child. Then Gerry arrived three years later. That was what they wanted, a son, someone to continue the Hogan name. Gerry and I were strong and healthy children,

Mr Freeman. When Gerry got the grades to get him to university, his future was guaranteed, and so was mine. My father was six years older than my mother; he retired two months after Gerry celebrated his eighteenth birthday at sixty-five. I quit my job with a bank in Church Street and stayed home to care for them. They diagnosed Dad with lung cancer while Gerry and Nick were away in Australia; Dad passed away fifteen months later. Mum reckoned he clung on until Gerry and Evelyn married. My mother died the year before Sean was born."

Gus had met dozens of women like Belinda Hogan. It was a generational thing. In other countries, the family unit was everything, regardless of the number of children and grandchildren. In the UK, until the end of WWII, it was common for parents to encourage a daughter to stay home to care for them. There was no opportunity for the girl to have a career. Sometimes it happened because the daughter didn't find a husband and got left behind. In other instances, they actively discouraged marriage.

Gus thought of Ursula Wakeley from Mere. Would she have died in such a terrible fashion if her parents had allowed her to continue working at the library, marry, and have children? In the last fifty years, daughters left home for university joined the armed forces and enjoyed careers in many professions. The idea of sacrificing their life to care for ageing parents no longer appealed. Why should it? There were so many broken homes, with families scattered across the globe, that most children, of whatever gender, couldn't wait to leave.

"Did Gerry have a temper?" asked Gus.

Belinda stopped twisting her handkerchief. Perhaps she expected Gus to sympathise with her lot. He did, but his focus was on finding her brother's killer.

"I can't recall a single occasion when Gerry got angry. It wasn't in his make-up."

"What about your father?" asked Gus.

"Dad was strict," said Belinda. "Both of our parents were strict. They didn't hit us if that's what you're driving at. We felt the lash of their tongue from time to time, usually with good reason. Gerry and I learned quickly not to step out of line."

"Nick Barrett told us that Gerry was anxious not to attract trouble," said Gus. "Yes, that fits in with the harsh schooling he endured in his formative years. He didn't want to upset his parents by getting into trouble and recognised that if he got a black mark on his character, then his planned successful career would disappear like smoke up a chimney."

"Nothing was going to stop Gerry from achieving that goal," said Belinda.

"Were you jealous of his success?" asked Blessing.

Belinda paused and looked directly at the young Detective Constable.

"I was proud of Gerry. Of course, I wished I had had the opportunity of a golden future as he did. If I was jealous, then what of it?"

"What were your first impressions of Evelyn?" asked Gus.

"Evelyn was beautiful," said Belinda. "I suppose you'll ask if I was jealous of her too? Evelyn was a tall, tanned Australian woman who loved to surf. She was self-confident, ambitious, and full of drive. Her career as a wildlife photographer was far removed from anything I could ever have hoped to tackle; it was laughable. So, of course, I was jealous. I wanted to hate her from the second she burst through the front door of this house with Gerry. He met her off the train just up the road from here. Evelyn had the guts to fly to England alone and take a train to the West Country to be with her man. Gerry had prayed they would meet again after he flew home in November with Nick Barrett."

"You said you wanted to hate her," said Gus.

"Evelyn sensed how I felt, totally ignored it, and wore me down. She mesmerised Gerry in Sydney and then did the same to our parents and me. Dad was glad for them to marry in a registry office despite only having known one another for weeks. If you had asked me before Gerry went abroad, I would have said my father would never have reacted that way in a million years. Dad's health had deteriorated so rapidly that he worried he wouldn't live to see it happen if they had a church wedding."

"You told us what happened over the next ten years," said Gus. "Gerry and Evelyn lived and worked in Bristol while you cared for your mother. Then, in 1992 they moved to Trowle Common, and sadly, you and Gerry lost your mother the following year. How did things change for you after you found yourself alone in this house?"

"Losing a parent is devastating," said Belinda, "but when my mother died, I lost so much more than Gerry. He had Evelyn, his job, and even his lifelong shadow, Nick Barrett. I had a few close friends and nothing more."

"Then Evelyn gave birth to Sean," said Gus. "A nephew."

"I offered to help at once," said Belinda. "Gerry was building his business. Evelyn wanted to continue to accept work in various parts of the country. She was freelance and very successful. Giving that up to care for Sean was not an option, even if they could have survived financially without her income. I had nothing but time on my hands."

"You provided free childcare," said Blessing.

"I was happy to do it. I had a purpose in life again."

"Within two years, you had another baby to care for," said Gus.

"Little Byron," said Belinda. "He was a treasure. They were both lovely children."

"Did Gerry and Evelyn spend much time with their sons?" asked Blessing.

"Gerry was always busy during the week. If Evelyn was away working, I brought the boys here. They slept in their father's old bedroom. Evelyn kept them with her at the Trowle house for the rest of the time. The boys rarely came here on the weekends. Gerry and Evelyn spent as much time with the boys as they could, given their busy lives."

"Many parents today struggle to pay for childcare," said Blessing. "How did you feel about not getting paid for the many hours you must have worked? Especially as you didn't have a job."

"That can be explained by the will, Blessing," said Gus.

"You're right, Mr Freeman," said Belinda. "When Dad died, everything passed to Mum. When Mum died, everything was to be split evenly between Gerry and me. In 1993, this house was worth a lot less than today, but I couldn't afford to give Gerry half. I needed my share of the rest of her estate to provide a modest income. The will stipulated that I should live here until I died, so our hands were tied. In other circumstances, I could have sold up, bought a smaller place on one of the new estates in town, and given Gerry his share. But my mother amended her will to give me the security of always having a roof over my head. It was her way of thanking me for giving up my hopes and ambitions to look after her and Dad. Mum knew Gerry was a wealthy man. He could afford to wait."

"Did you and Evelyn meet up often?" asked Gus.

"We didn't have coffee mornings or do lunch, if that's what you mean. I saw Evelyn when she dropped the boys here on her way to the airport or when I returned them to Trowle Common a day or two later. Evelyn spent any spare time she had with Gerry and the boys."

"So, she never mentioned that a charity based in New South Wales offered her a well-paid job three months before she returned to Macquarie Pass for the last time?"

"No, she didn't," said Belinda. "Nor did Gerry."

"Evelyn turned them down," said Gus, "but she hoped that trip was the first step in making a permanent move back to Australia."

"I don't believe you. Evelyn was happy here. She loved Gerry and the boys. Gerry had given her everything she asked for with the improvements to the house."

"Sorry," said Gus. "I meant that the trip was a first step in moving the family back to her homeland. Evelyn wanted her boys to grow up on the beach in the sun, not the grey, damp winters of the UK. She reasoned that with the internet, Gerry could run his financial business from anywhere in the world."

"Well, that's the first time I've heard that. Did Gerry know? Was he in favour?"

"We don't know, Ms Hogan," said Gus. "How would you have reacted to that news if you'd learned it in 2001?"

"It would have been devastating," said Belinda. "I would have hated to see my boys disappear to the other side of the world. I don't know what I would have done."

"Where were you when Gerry received news of Evelyn's death?" asked Gus.

"Evelyn's car crashed over the safety barrier after she'd finished work for the day," said Belinda. "Over here, that was at seven in the morning. The boys were staying with me. I got them ready for school, and they left the house at the usual time. The police called Gerry at the office at one o'clock in the afternoon. He came straight here with the news. He was in tears. We collected the boys from school together. It was a dreadful time."

"I can imagine," said Gus.

"Gerry flew out to Sydney and met with Evelyn's parents," said Belinda.

She struggled to contain her emotions.

"Nick Barrett has told us the details, Ms Hogan," said Blessing. "There's no need to distress yourself. Gerry and Evelyn's parents scattered her ashes in the park."

"You cared for the boys while Gerry was in Australia," said Gus. "He didn't return until the middle of March, I believe?"

"That's right," said Belinda. "It was just the three of us for weeks. A sad yet happy time."

"Nick Barrett told us that when Gerry got home, he tried to be a brilliant father to Sean and Byron."

"I thought he would throw himself into his work to cope with the loss of Evelyn, but he spent every spare minute with those boys. There were still times during the week that Gerry needed my help, but he devoted his weekends to Sean and Byron."

"He met Rachel Cummins five years after Evelyn's death," said Gus. "That seems a reasonable length of time to wait before moving on."

"That woman was almost twenty years younger than Gerry. What could they possibly have in common? Evelyn was a renowned wildlife photographer. I don't think a fitness trainer has the same gravitas, do you? Gerry ran a successful professional firm. He deserved a better class of person by his side."

"You filled that role to some extent for the previous five years," said Blessing. "You must have been annoyed."

"Annoyed? I was livid," said Belinda. "After everything that I'd done for him. The first pretty girl to flash her eyes at him, and Gerry jumps into bed with her. A leopard doesn't change its spots."

"Gerry certainly had a few girlfriends over the years," said Gus.

"Not while he and Evelyn were married; he didn't," said Belinda. "Why couldn't he see that Sean and Byron were happy with having their Dad's attention far more than they ever had, plus the love of their Auntie Belinda? They knew they could wrap me around their little finger, but I would have done anything for them."

"Gerry needed something that you couldn't give him," said Blessing.

"I'm sure he could have found someone his own age," said Belinda.

"Rachel Cummins told us that there was an instant attraction between her and Gerry," said Gus.

"Huh! She saw a meal ticket. Gerry was a widower who ran his own firm. She made a few phone calls, asked her clients for information, and discovered Gerry Hogan had money and property. Gerry was vulnerable. An old fool hypnotised by a young, firm body."

"Things must have changed for you when Rachel moved in with Gerry?" asked Gus.

"They had changed already, Mr Freeman," said Belinda. "Sean was thirteen and Byron eleven. They didn't need their Auntie Belinda as much. Gerry never left them alone at weekends. They went everywhere together—Foot-ball, cricket, rugby, stately homes, country parks, and the seaside. There was the snooker, too, even before Byron became so good. They played at home and then attended matches at various venues around the country whenever they could."

"After Rachel moved in, Gerry extended the kitchen and added the gym," said Gus. "Did you ever get to see those improvements?"

"That Cummins woman would never invite me over," said Belinda. "I didn't go there more than a handful of times when Evelyn was alive, but I saw what Gerry had done to the place. I often dropped in after Evelyn died because the boys had so many things at the house. They didn't like my small TV when they had satellite TV at home. I didn't have the computer games they enjoyed either. You know what teenagers are like these days."

"Not in a domestic situation," said Gus. "I meet them when they've broken the law."

"You never had cause to visit Trowle Common while Rachel lived there?" asked Blessing.

"Why did I need a reason?" asked Belinda. "Gerry was my only brother. Sean and Byron are my nephews. No, Rachel turned Gerry against me."

"Let's turn our attention to May the sixth, 2012," said Gus. "Where were you that night?"

"I was here watching TV. Alone, as usual."

"When did you hear Gerry was dead?"

"Not on Sunday evening," said Belinda. "I didn't hear until almost lunchtime on Monday."

"Rachel found Gerry's body outside the house at a quarter to seven," said Gus. "Her screams brought Sean and Byron to the door."

"Typical of the woman," said Belinda. "They should never have been allowed to see their father like that. They had already had to suffer the trauma of losing their mother."

"Rachel told Sean to call the emergency services," said Gus. "Nobody called you; Gerry's only blood relative?"

"The police stood by until the paramedics had left and then got the body moved to the morgue. It was too late to do much more that night. DS Bennison phoned on Monday to arrange to speak with me. She told me the terrible news and took my statement."

"That's still a long time, Ms Hogan," said Gus. "I wonder why Sean or Byron didn't call?"

"No doubt Rachel Cummins put a stop to it. The poor things must have been traumatised. They needed their Auntie Belinda, just like they did after their mother died."

"When did you meet with DI Kirkpatrick?" asked Gus.

"The female detective who first phoned me was more sensible. She understood what I was going through. Her boss, however, didn't listen to a thing I said. I told him on Tuesday evening to look more closely at Rachel Cummins. She must have paid someone to shoot Gerry. Now you're looking into the murder again and making the same mistakes. I suppose she has you wrapped around her little finger, too, just like she had Gerry. Who benefitted from his death? As soon as that woman had persuaded Gerry to alter his will, that sealed his fate. It stands to reason."

"Let's consider those points one at a time, Ms Hogan," said Gus. "John Kirkpatrick checked into Rachel Cummins and everyone else that had links to Gerry. I've not met a hired killer yet who does a job without payment. They checked Ms Cummins's bank account, looking for evidence of large bank transfers or cash withdrawals. They found nothing. We're taking a fresh look at Gerry's death, but we're not religiously following the same lines of enquiry that

Kirkpatrick and Bennison followed six years ago. Rachel Cummins gets treated in the same way as any witness. We don't have favourites nor give anyone a free pass."

"That's as maybe, but there's no getting around the will," said Belinda.

"You asked who benefitted," said Gus. "Well, you did, Ms Hogan. You received the sum of two hundred thousand pounds, I believe? Gerry recognised the love you had lavished on his boys whenever the need arose. That bequest allowed you to improve your annual income. The monies held in trust for Sean and Byron are due on their twenty-fifth birthday. No doubt that will be welcome news for Sean if he's thinking of getting married to Clare. What a great start to their married life. Byron is attempting to hit the heights in a profession where he can travel thousands of miles to play in a tournament, only to lose in the first round and earn nothing. Both boys will need a place of their own one day. Gerry set them up to receive a tidy sum when they were old enough to use it wisely."

"Gerry left her the house," said Belinda. "That's an awful lot of money for just five years keeping a middle-aged man happy."

"You haven't stepped inside that home for years, Ms Hogan," said Gus. "Gerry kept Evelyn's studio locked. Nothing was ever to be touched. He added the sunroom and games room at the rear for all the family, but two rooms on the ground floor were Evelyn's domain. Rachel never goes there. Every time she steps outside the front door, the nightmare returns. I doubt Sean and Byron will ever erase the memory of their father sprawled on the gravel that night. When the boys get settled, Rachel will sell up and move somewhere smaller. Gerry left her that option. No matter what you think of her, Ms Hogan, she's considered the feelings of those boys every step of the way."

"So, she'll get away with murder. I might have known. Another man blinded by her good looks."

"We follow the evidence, Ms Hogan," said Blessing. "No matter how much you want it to be the case, there's nothing to suggest that Rachel Cummins had anything to do with your brother's death."

"DC Umeh is correct," said Gus. "We keep probing for the truth in this case. Everyone we've spoken to paints the same picture of Gerry Hogan. Either they're all lying, or he really was a saint. I've been at this game for a long time, Ms Hogan. It's rare for me to fail to spot a crack in the different accounts people provide. Why would Nick Barrett lie about a man who was his only real friend? Why would Rachel Cummins lie about the man she loved? Now you, Ms Hogan. You don't have a high opinion of Gerry's best friend, Nick. You think even less of Rachel. However, your account of everything that Gerry did, from his schooldays to the day he died, matches what we've heard from the others. Ever since I started looking into this case, I've been searching for a person, an event, an argument, or something that might have lit the fuse that led to Gerry getting shot. Where else is there is his life left to look?"

"You'll never shake my belief that that woman was behind it, Mr Freeman," said Belinda Hogan.

She stood and waited. Gus realised Belinda believed this meeting would serve no useful purpose. He decided there was little point in asking her further questions. They needed to meet with Sean Hogan and then get back to the office to check on the Hub's progress. The truths he sought had to lie somewhere.

Gus and Blessing walked into the hallway in silence.

Belinda Hogan opened the front door and watched them set off towards the river bridge. After they disappeared around the corner, she entered her lounge and picked up her mobile phone.

"Sean? It's Auntie Belinda. Hello, darling, how are you? Watch yourself this afternoon. The police are intent on a cover-up again. They'll write off your father's murder as a mystery they couldn't unravel, and we'll never know the truth."

Chapter Ten

"I CAN SEE why you walked out on her, guv," said Blessing.

"We had little choice, Blessing," said Gus. "I thought it best to avoid antagonising her further by saying we might be back with more questions."

"Is it possible that everyone is lying, guv?"

"I don't think so," said Gus. "You get a feeling for a witness in the first few minutes of meeting them. Nobody I've spoken to this week struck me as trying to hide something. I accepted Nick Barrett's words as gospel. Rachel Cummins also seemed an honest person to Luke and me. As for Belinda Hogan, she's evenly balanced with a chip on both shoulders. Her parents started her descent into the bitter woman she is today. I wonder what the customers at that bank where she worked thought of the eighteen-year-old cashier that greeted them with a smile every morning? A decade later, she was housebound with an ailing mother. Then a light shone in her life. Sean and Byron needed a nanny so Evelyn could continue pursuing her career. After Evelyn's death, Belinda expected Gerry to rely on her even more; instead, he did his utmost to be a father and mother to the boys. Belinda's hopes got crushed after Rachel and Gerry met. Losing Gerry was the final straw."

"Belinda ignored your point about the money Gerry left her, didn't she, guv?"

"I don't think the money was the issue, Blessing," said Gus. "I expect Gerry told her about the will he made after Evelyn died. He wanted to ensure the boys' future after his death. They were only eight and six at the time of that car crash."

"Belinda would have been their parent and guardian until they reached the age of majority," said Blessing.

"That situation changed when Gerry met Rachel, but Belinda didn't know."

They reached the station car park and got into Gus's car. Gus eased the Focus into the lunchtime traffic and drove towards Trowbridge.

"Isn't this the wrong way, guv?" Blessing asked.

"It will be simpler to stay close to Bradford-on-Avon," said Gus. "We need to be at the Hogan company offices by two o'clock. I prefer to pop into town for a snack, and we can continue to mull over the case while we make our way back. We'll pass the Hogan house on Trowle Common going this way. I'll point it out to you."

Gus hoped that Blessing enjoyed the type of snacks that Gregg's offered.

He needn't have worried. As Gus drove them back towards Bradford, Blessing set the ball rolling.

"You've handled more murder cases than I have, guv," she said. "Do you know what would help in this case?"

"A miracle?" asked Gus.

"Perhaps. All the people I want to speak to are dead. Nick Barrett told you everything that happened while he and Gerry Hogan were at university or on that trip to Australia. You believed him. I want to ask Gerry if what his friend said was accurate."

"Well, we might be able to speak to other students," said Gus. "Or a few of the girls Gerry knew in Australia."

"Then there's Evelyn. She knew Gerry best. They were married for twenty years. If there were something iffy about Nick's story, she would point it out. Evelyn knew Belinda for the longest time, too, so she could put you right if there were gaps in her sister-in-law's account."

"I can see where you're going with this, Blessing," said Gus. "If we could only ask Gerry whether he ever wondered if Rachel was after his money, it might add strength to Belinda's fanciful scenario. It is what it is, Blessing. Until I came out of retirement to head up the Crime Review Team, my murders were 'live' investigations. I was the first detective to try to solve the riddle. It was rare for other family members or witnesses to die before I could corroborate another person's statement."

"You and the team have dealt with cases where the gap has been greater than six years, guv. It feels with this case as though there are more deaths and more uncorroborated statements than the norm."

"I can't argue with that, Blessing," said Gus.

"We've still got forty minutes, guv,"

"We'll park the car, get a coffee and walk to the Marina. Neil tells me it's a pleasant spot to sit and watch the world go by."

"A marina? Are we back to the canal again, guv?"

"The Kennet and Avon, the one that linked with the waterway in Swindon where they found Stacey Reade's body. The Bradford Marina is less than a ten-minute walk from the car park, and Sean Hogan's office is near the marina."

"There's a method in your madness," said Blessing.

"I do try, Blessing. Although, this case is driving me mad. Let's see if we can find the coffee house that Neil mentioned."

Blessing walked beside her boss as they entered a narrow street.

"This is quaint, guv. It reminds me of Diagon Alley."

"Really, where's that, Warwick?"

"It doesn't matter, guv."

"This place is The Shambles, Blessing."

"We can always try somewhere else, guv."

"That's the name of the street, Blessing. It's full of old-world charm and sits on the site of the medieval market stalls. This would have been an open space in the early Middle Ages, except on market days, when traders could set up their stalls. Gradually the stalls became permanent structures and were replaced by buildings, some of which remain. Like that pair of houses with timber fronts we can see on the other side of the street. They're also from the fifteenth century. Their cellars were once the town's lockup."

"You know a lot about the history of Bradford-on-Avon, guv."

"You can thank Neil for that, Blessing. He couldn't resist telling me everything he'd learned on a visit with Melody."

They found the coffee house and soon went to the canal towpath. Neil was right. It was a quiet refuge in the heart of the town, and there were several spare benches for them to watch the passing traffic.

"Why do men of a certain age insist on lycra, guv?" asked Blessing as a grey-haired cyclist pedalled past them.

"No comment," said Gus. A female jogger with an inadequate sports bra headed slowly in the opposite direction.

"This spot is a magnet for families during the school holidays, guv," said Blessing.

"Too many people dashing to and fro to get the full effect of life on the canal," said Gus. "When you watch the canal boats negotiating the lock over there inching towards Avoncliff, you can appreciate the true meaning of leisure."

"We won't find you jogging or cycling shortly then, guv?"

"Not likely. Suzie has tried to persuade me to join her on her weekly horseback ride. A gentle hack around the lanes and tracks between Worton and Urchfont. That's more appealing."

"Of course, it is guv. You get to spend more time with DI Ferris. You should go for it."

"Has Jackie ever tried to tempt you? They have several horses in the stables."

"They frighten me, guv," said Blessing. "I'm not a country girl like DI Ferris."

"Finished your coffee?" asked Gus. Blessing nodded and placed the cup in Gus's outstretched hand. He walked to the other side of the towpath to put their cups in the waste bin.

"Look out, guv!" cried Blessing. "Skateboard alert!"

Gus managed to avoid the teenage skater who trundled past. There was no point shouting after him with the outsized headphones he wore.

"I'd better watch where I'm walking," said Gus. "Right, let's get back to the main road. It's safer."

They soon found the offices of Hogan Finance, established in 1992, and entered the reception area. A smartly dressed young woman looked up and greeted them with a beaming smile.

"Good afternoon. I'm Emma. How can I help you today?"

"We're Mr Hogan's two o'clock appointment," said Gus. "Mr Freeman and DC Umeh."

"One moment. I'll tell Mr Hogan that you've arrived."

Gus quickly took in his surroundings. One girl in reception. Two offices on the ground floor. He wondered who occupied the upper floor.

"The entrance must be at the rear, guv," whispered Blessing. "There's an alleyway to the right-hand side of this building. No stairs are visible here, so they must be behind a false wall with an access point directly overhead. She wandered across to her left and knocked on the wall. The hollow sound brought a massive smile from Blessing.

"Not very often that I'm wrong," she said, "but I'm right again."

"Mr Hogan will see you now,"

Emma had returned from the larger office of the two.

Gus and Blessing walked in to meet the current head of Hogan Finance.

Sean Hogan looked totally at ease in his surroundings.

His office was light and airy, fitted with every gadget the modern CEO could want. Gus wondered how his father had looked at twenty-four years of age. Gerry returned from Australia in November 1981, got married early in the New Year, lived in Clifton, and learned the finance business at the sharp end with a newly formed company. Gus doubted that Gerry would look this cool.

"Come in. Please take a seat. When one of your colleagues called, he said you were opening the file again on my father's murder."

"We never close the file until we've found the killer, Mr Hogan," said Gus.

"Right. So, what do you need from me?"

"I have a basic understanding of what you do here, Mr Hogan," said Gus. "Has it altered much since your father's death? Are you taking the business in a different direction?"

"Dad followed basic principles," said Scan. "Daniel got schooled in the same manner, and I can't see any good reason to change the range of products we offer. The packaging might get a revamp from time to time, but the core elements remain. Everyone has a different vision of their ideal future, Mr Freeman. That's why we at Hogan's work hard to understand clients' life goals. I need to get to know the real person to help build a unique financial plan that delivers the lifestyle they have in mind. I want to know their needs, goals, and approach to risk. Some people are already planning their ideal future, but you would be surprised how many have made no plans whatsoever. For instance, a quick look at your current arrangements would enable me to see whether they're likely to deliver the goods."

"I'm not here to discuss my arrangements," said Gus. "When your father set up this business, did he handle everything in-house?"

"He came here from Hargreaves Lansdown, as I'm sure you know," said Sean. "He left there with their good wishes, and there were no issues with him branching out on his own. My father understood how to advise on various investment services and products. He used managers from across the fund management industry to help him meet his client's needs in those early years. People that he believed possessed the right skills and expertise. As the years passed, Dad needed to rely on those managers less and less."

"You don't employ many members of staff," said Gus. "Your set-up is more of a lean, mean fighting machine."

"Which is precisely the model my father wanted," said Sean.

"Did you ever take an interest in your late mother's work? Did she show you how to use a camera, for example?"

"I was only eight when Mum died, Mr Freeman. The kit she used was far too specialised for us boys. We each had a 'point and shoot' cheap camera for days out with our parents. Mum died before we were able to appreciate just how good she was. Her studio was off-limits then, and it still is today. I would love to see her portfolio find a wider market. Her photographs appeared in dozens of magazines and periodicals. Maybe one day, I'll ask Byron to take a look. He's the artistic one. Perhaps he could catalogue her work and publish it in a book. My role would be to find the best place to invest the proceeds."

"You both spent a good deal of time with your Aunt, didn't you?" asked Blessing.

"Both before Mum died and afterwards. Yes, we couldn't have got through it without her. Mum's death devastated Dad. He was operating on auto-pilot for months. He spent much more time with Byron and me, ensuring we were okay. He was a laugh."

"Really," said Gus. "The people we've spoken to have told us what a great chap he was, but I can't recall anyone mentioning his sense of humour."

"You know that Byron is a professional snooker player?"

Gus nodded.

"Well, I started playing at eight. Dad had always played. Nick Barrett played with Dad at the club on Market Street."

"We know it," said Gus. "One of my sergeants went there the other evening."

"Dad showed me the rudiments of the game, and we

had a knockabout on the table in the games room. Byron was too short to be able to join in at six years old, so Dad got him a stool. Byron was a natural, and Dad spotted his potential. Did you ever watch John Virgo on TV?"

"I don't recognise the name, sorry," said Gus.

"He was a professional player who still commentates on the game. Dad told us that the pros would go to small clubs like the one in town and play exhibition matches in the old days. Those nights supplemented their income in the days before colour television. It was hard to sell the game to TV companies when everything was black and white. Anyway, there weren't as many tournaments as there are today. Virgo wasn't the best player, so he covered his blunder with a joke when one of his trick shots went wrong. As time went by, the routine was more comedy than trick shots as he entertained the crowds with impersonations of top players, past and present."

"Did your father have a talent for impressions?" asked Gus.

"Not really. Dad was hopeless. But for us boys, it was great spending time with him. By the time Rachel moved in, it was obvious Byron could be an exceptional player."

"Did Rachel ever join in?" asked Blessing.

"She used the time to work out in the gym Dad had installed for her. Rachel stuck her head around the door to call us for dinner or ask when we were going to bed on a school night. She never wanted to play."

"What did she think of your Dad playing the fool?" asked Blessing.

"Dad wouldn't have let anyone else see him like that," said Sean. "He used to tell us there was a time for business and a time for fun. He let his hair down for a few minutes in that games room and had us in stitches. As soon as we walked back into the lounge or the kitchen, he was back to his usual, sober self."

"When did Byron start playing in the snooker club?" asked Gus.

"I had to be sixteen before they allowed me to become a member," said Sean, "but the committee listened to Nick Barrett's advice that they could benefit from encouraging a special talent to blossom. Byron played his first tournament there soon after his fourteenth birthday."

"That was in 2010?" asked Gus.

"That's right. Byron won that tournament, and everyone sat up and took notice. Nick Barrett was right. The club's image went up several notches, and better players from the region applied to join."

"You continued to play at home, just the three of you?" asked Blessing.

"Yes, we did. Because Dad could tell that Byron needed to get used to proper match conditions, he tried to make things in the games room as authentic as possible. When the three of us played together, one acted as a referee and marker. Dad bought a pair of white gloves. While I watched Byron compile yet another hundred break against me, Dad pretended to be Jan Verhaas, the Dutch referee. He'd been on the World Snooker scene since 2003. Dad was tall and distinguished-looking, like 'Jan the Man', and he'd try to get the accent right when he called out the break. They were the happiest times I remember. Byron will say the same."

"How did you react to your father's relationship with Rachel?" asked Blessing.

"It was awkward at first," said Sean. "When Mum died, it felt like we'd never get over it. I cried for weeks. Aunt Belinda had always been part of our family and did her best to fill the gap, but she wasn't Mum. It was Dad who changed the most. He spent every minute of his free time with Byron and me. He never took us anywhere with Aunt Belinda. When he met Rachel, they just clicked. Byron and I were too young to understand what was going on, but from the start, Dad included Rachel. We met her at a restaurant first, then a month or two later we went abroad on holiday together. A week in Portugal. After that, Rachel moved in with us. Rachel made Dad happy. She was always good to us, and she never tried to become our Mum. She told us when we were on that holiday always to call her Rachel."

"The awkwardness soon disappeared, and you never doubted that she loved your Dad?" asked Blessing.

"Never," said Sean. "Aunt Belinda got it into her head that Rachel wasn't good enough for Dad. The more she tried to split them up, the less time Dad had for her. So dad continued spending as much time with us as possible, and Rachel took the slack. Aunt Belinda wasn't needed to babysit us anymore. I was thirteen when Rachel moved in. Dad only went out during the evening when Rachel hadn't a fitness class. I went into the games room with Byron or watched TV with Rachel."

"Are you able to talk us through events on the evening your Dad died?" asked Gus.

"I think so," said Sean. "I've been through it enough times this past six years. But I'll never forget it. Dad told us after Mum died that there was no time limit on grief."

"Was it a typical Sunday?"

"We had decided to spend the weekend at home because of the World Snooker Final. So we watched TV for long periods on Saturdays. Then, whenever there was an interval, we dashed into the games room to play a few frames. We had a late breakfast on Sunday, watched the afternoon session, and Rachel cooked a meal for us at around five o'clock."

"Was that normal?" asked Blessing.

"No, we often ate at lunchtime, especially when the four of us went out for the afternoon and evening. Dad thought it gave us more time to play snooker before the evening session started."

"You were in the games room when the front doorbell rang at six-thirty," said Gus. "Why didn't one of you answer?"

"Byron saw the light flashing," said Sean. "It distracted him, and he missed the last red. The black was on its spot, and he only needed the yellow for another century. He swore. Dad told him off. The light didn't flash again, so we thought they'd either gone away or Rachel had answered. But, instead, she was in the gym working on a new routine."

"Did you have a TV in the games room?" asked Blessing.

"Yes, a small one. We usually tuned it to one of the sports channels with the sound off."

"You said earlier that you watched TV in the lounge with Rachel."

"We did," said Sean. "Rachel enjoyed all sorts of shows. Comedies, dramas, quizzes. We didn't watch sport twenty-four seven."

"What happened then?" asked Gus.

"I kept an eye on the screen while Byron was racking the balls for a new frame. I saw Ronnie O'Sullivan leaving his dressing-room. The camera tracked him to the top of the stairs, where the MC did the big build-up to bring the players into the arena. Ali Carter was just leaving his dressing room. I knew Dad wanted to see the whole session, so I gave him a call."

"What could you see in the hallway?"

"Nothing, except the front door was partly closed. I went back to the games room to watch the build-up."

"Then what happened?"

"The next thing I heard was this dreadful scream. Byron and I ran into the hallway. The front door was wide open, and Rachel was on her knees, cradling Dad's head in her lap. There was blood everywhere. We couldn't move. I remember grabbing Byron's hand and clinging to him for dear life. Not again, I thought. We'd lost Mum, and now Dad was dead."

"Did you hear the gunshot?" asked Gus.

"We didn't hear a thing," said Sean. "Byron had turned up the volume on the TV, and when the door was closed, it was difficult to hear anything outside. That's why Dad put in the lighting system. The sunroom, games room, and Mum's studio had soundproofing. Dad wanted everyone to have quiet when they were working or relaxing."

"You were certain that your Dad was dead?" asked Blessing.

"The wound to his head," said Sean. "It was awful."

"What did Rachel say to you?"

"She told me to call 999."

"Why did you ask for an ambulance and the police if you were sure he was dead?"

"Rachel told me to call them."

"How long was it before they arrived at the house?"

"The paramedics were there first, ten minutes later. Then the police car drove through the gateway. Another six or seven minutes, perhaps."

"Did you and Byron stand in the doorway all that time? Except for when you used the landline to call the emergency services."

"No. A uniformed officer took us inside. She sat with us in the lounge."

"I'm sorry we made you go through that ordeal again," said Gus. "I know it was the millionth time you've done it. Was there anything different on this occasion?"

Sean shook his head.

"An unusual evening," said Gus. "Not the same routine that you followed on other Sundays. Yet surely, several things stayed the same? The three of you were in the games room. Byron was playing you off the table, and Dad was refereeing. I've seen the crime scene photographs. Where were the white gloves?"

"Was he wearing them when he left the games room?" asked Blessing.

"Yes," said Sean, "now you mention it. Yes, he was. It was second nature by that time. He must have forgotten he was wearing them."

"We'll check with Rachel," said Gus. "Maybe your Dad took them off."

"If he'd stuffed them in his pocket, guv," said Blessing. "The police would have found them later. They would have listed the gloves among his belongings."

"True. Rachel might have found them near the porch," said Gus. "Perhaps, Gerry discarded them somewhere while he spoke to the visitor, intending to pick them up on his way indoors."

"Byron might remember something that I don't," said Sean. "With the shock of seeing Dad that way, I might not have noticed the gloves were missing before I made the phone call. Until you asked just now, I hadn't given them a thought."

"Thank you for your time, Mr Hogan," said Gus. "We'll let you get on with your day. You've been most helpful. The white gloves could be the first fresh lead we've found since we started."

"I'm not sure how the gloves could lead you to Dad's killer, Mr Freeman," said Sean.

"Nor do I," said Gus, "but for some reason, I feel more positive than I did before we spoke with you."

"When is Byron due back in this country?" asked Blessing.

"If he keeps winning matches, he'll play in the final on Sunday and fly back to Bristol on Monday. Then, I can give him a ring and say you want to talk to him at the house on Monday evening. Is that okay?"

"We'll put the date in our diary," said Blessing. "What if he loses before then?"

Sean grinned.

"He'll fly back at the weekend but won't want to chat. He's not used to losing."

"If our other enquiries push us in a different direction, we may need to reschedule anyway," said Gus. "Will Byron fly out for another tournament later next week?"

"I think they're off to China at the weekend."

Gus and Blessing left the office and met the ever-smiling Emma in the reception area.

"Thank you for visiting Hogan Finance. Enjoy the rest of your day."

Gus wasn't interested in financial affairs. He was interested in a pair of white gloves.

Chapter Eleven

"THAT WAS A SURPRISE, GUV," said Blessing.

"Back to the car, Blessing," said Gus. "The game's afoot. Those gloves are the first thing that has differed from the first investigation. Kirkpatrick didn't find them. We'll check with Rachel Cummins."

"If Rachel didn't rescue them from the porch, where could they have gone?" asked Blessing. She had to hurry to keep up with her boss. He was on a mission.

"Rachel wouldn't have removed them from Gerry's hands, surely, guv?"

"If she was traumatised by what she found outside the door? Who knows what either of us would do in those circumstances?"

"I reckon the killer took them," said Blessing. "He needed to ditch the gun. He used the gloves to wipe the weapon clean of fingerprints."

"That's a possibility," said Gus. "Rachel would spot their visitor was already wearing gloves. It was a pleasantly warm evening in early May."

They reached the station car park. Gus sat inside the Focus and waited for Blessing to get comfortable.

He drove out of Bradford-on-Avon and headed for the office.

"A helmet, gloves, and leathers are de rigueur for a moped, let alone a proper motorcycle," said Gus. "Our witness said it sounded like an angry wasp. It always seemed that any bike the neighbour heard was something a kid rode, not an adult male. I'm more convinced than ever that it's irrelevant."

"The man was casually dressed, guv, not in motorcycle gear," said Blessing. "If he intended to confront Gerry Hogan and shoot him, he would want to be in and out of that driveway in seconds. He must have arrived at the house by another means."

"How far was it to walk to the house from the nearest bus stop?" asked Gus, "Buses do run out to Trowle Common. Could he have walked to the house, shot Gerry, and then taken the gloves with him?"

"It would have been simple enough to pull the gloves from Gerry's hands," said Blessing. "Then run away, clean the gun, drop it into a drain, and make his way back to Trowbridge or on to Bradford-on-Avon. He could have dropped the white gloves in the first waste bin he saw."

"It's a theory, Blessing," said Gus. "We'll test it when we've got the answers we want from Rachel and Byron."

"Although…" said Blessing.

"Go on," said Gus, "What doesn't fit?"

"Why take both gloves? The killer only needed one to remove his fingerprints. Why waste the extra few seconds it took to remove the second glove? In fact, why not leave the gloves where they were and use them to clean the gun?"

Gus pondered the scene for a few seconds.

"No, that won't work. The killer needed something to help disguise the gun as he escaped. How would he carry it without leaving evidence or risking it getting spotted? There's something else that's troubling me."

"What's that, guv?" asked Blessing.

"If this were a hired assassin, he would prepare beforehand. He wouldn't stand on the doorstep working out what to do next."

"It was always possible it was someone with a grievance," said Blessing. "Someone that Gerry had pushed to the brink. They could have panicked if they were the first time they'd fired a gun."

"That's more than likely," said Gus. "It opens up another possibility, Blessing. The gun was there to threaten Gerry Hogan, but murder was never part of the plan. Our surprised killer had a dead body at his feet and a smoking gun. The gloves provided a temporary cover, plus a way of wiping the weapon clean. The rest of the picture we painted still holds good. He ran off, cleaned the gun and dropped it down a drain."

Gus rapped the steering wheel.

"I knew there was something funny about that gun."

"Why, guv," asked Blessing.

"There was only one shot fired. That was what the neighbour heard. Forget the motorcycle backfiring. That's rubbish. When the council operative discovered the gun five months later, it was empty. It only ever had one bullet in it."

"That begs another question, guv," said Blessing. "If murder wasn't on that man's mind, why bother with ammunition?"

They arrived in the Old Police Station car park, and Gus parked the car.

"Have I made things worse, guv?" asked Blessing as they entered the lift.

"Our first job is to ask Rachel Cummins about the gloves," said Gus.

The rest of the team was spinning their wheels, waiting for information from the Hub.

"We've heard nothing yet, guv," said Luke. "They promised something by close of play today."

"Did you two make any progress?" asked Alex.

"White gloves," said Blessing. "Sean Hogan told us his Dad wore white gloves when refereeing frames between him and Byron. We're checking whether Gerry Hogan wore them when he stepped outside the house."

"He wasn't wearing gloves when he died," said Lydia, looking at the crime scene photos on the wallboard.

"Ah," said Blessing. "He might have been. The killer could have removed them."

Neil Davis gave a low whistle.

"Either he was a cool customer, or something went wrong,"

Blessing nodded. Gus was still talking on the phone.

"We can't ask Byron whether he remembers the gloves until he gets home from his latest snooker tournament," she said.

"Who's he playing this week, Blessing," asked Neil. "Is it the Russian billiards player, In- off the Red?"

"I don't know the names of any professionals," said Blessing.

"Some fall on stony ground, Neil," said Alex.

Gus ended the call and leaned back in his chair.

"Right, I don't know how much Blessing has told you of what we learned from Belinda and Sean Hogan, but this case could have just turned on its head."

"If it's a positive turn, I'm in favour, guv," said Luke.

"Rachel Cummins has just told me she didn't pick up any white gloves on the porch," said Gus. "She was adamant that Gerry wasn't wearing gloves."

"Is she suggesting Sean was mistaken, guv?" asked Neil.

"Not at all. Sean told us Gerry wasn't the only one to wear the gloves. They took turns when they refereed a frame to replicate what Byron would experience in his career as closely as possible. It was one of many examples of coaching him on the road to becoming world champion."

"What next, guv?" asked Luke.

"Sean knows we wish to speak to Byron. I'm hoping he hasn't rung him already and mentioned those gloves. I want to get to him before he's aware of what Sean told us."

"We have a contact number for a World Snooker representative, guv," said Luke. "Shall I try to get through to Byron this afternoon?"

"You can try, Luke. Sean mentioned China next weekend. They're playing in Europe somewhere this week. At least we shouldn't need to get Byron out of bed."

"Unless he's a chip off the old block," said Lydia.

Luke made the call.

"We'll update our files," said Gus. "The rest of you will need to wait until tomorrow morning to have time to read through what the two of us learned. When did you last give the Hub a nudge, Lydia?"

"It's only half-past three, guv. Divya said we'd get the information by five."

"I'm not hanging around until five to find they're sat on their backsides thinking they can afford to wait until the morning before getting in touch. Get on the phone. Tell them we need it pronto."

"Yes, guv," said Lydia.

"Any luck, Luke?" asked Gus.

"Byron's match in the last sixteen was this afternoon, guv. He won four frames to one. He won't play his quarter-final until tomorrow evening. You should receive a phone call from him at his hotel in Antalya in fifteen minutes."

"Excellent," said Gus. "We might get one thing cleared up before we go home."

Gus started keying in his notes from the interviews with Belinda and Sean Hogan.

"Divya apologises for the delay, guv, but one server has been down this morning," said Lydia. "We should hear about Gerry's girls by lunchtime tomorrow. However, the forensic accounting routines carried on without interruption. Since Gerry Hogan started the business, Hogan Finance has been as clean as a whistle."

"Thank you, Lydia," said Gus. "Well, that puts another loose end to bed. If his killer had a grievance, it had nothing to do with how Gerry handled his money."

Blessing wondered what Gus would do if Divya came up empty-handed.

Gus's phone rang fifteen minutes later.

"Turkish delight, I wonder?" he said before picking up.

"Good afternoon, Byron. Gus Freeman here, from Wiltshire Police. I don't know if you've heard from Sean."

"No, sir," replied Byron.

"Well, my colleague DS Sherman contacted you earlier in the week to explain what we're doing. As I told Sean this afternoon, no case is ever closed. We didn't find your father's killer six years ago, but we could be closer to the truth now. I don't need to trawl through the same ground I went over with your brother. I wish you to tell me one thing, and one thing only. Remember when your Dad heard

Rachel call him on that Sunday night. Remind me, where were you?"

"In the games room. We were playing a few frames before the evening session started."

"You were playing Sean, is that right, and Dad was the referee?"

"That's right."

"You heard Rachel call out. Then what happened?"

"Dad went to see who it was at the front door."

"Did he do anything before he left?"

"He told me off for swearing. The amber light flashing put me off. I got into perfect position on the final black, but the red wobbled."

"Nothing else?"

"No. Why?"

"So Dad still wore his white referee gloves?"

"He must have. Dad didn't remove them. I'm positive. I can see him now, wagging a finger at me because I swore."

"That's fine, Byron," said Gus. "That was what we needed to know. I hear you won this afternoon, is the tournament going well?"

"I played poorly and won today," said Byron. "I'll have to up my game tomorrow night if I want to be around at the weekend."

"Good luck," said Gus. "We might pop over to Trowle Common for a chat next week before you fly out again."

Gus ended the call.

"Listen up," he said. "Let's run through our revised scenario. Gerry is outside with a stranger just after six-thirty. Gerry is casually dressed and wearing a pair of white gloves. The stranger has a weapon containing a single bullet. There's an argument, and the gun gets fired. Gerry falls to the ground, fatally wounded. Rachel hears Sean calling for his father and leaves the gym at six forty-five. When she opens the front door, the stranger has gone. Gerry is dead and no longer wearing the gloves. What happened?"

"The gunman took them," said Alex, "but why?"

"Over to you, Blessing," said Gus.

"If there was a motorcycle in the area that evening, it had nothing to do with the murder," said Blessing. "If someone who wanted Gerry dead hired a killer, they would have expected them to prepare for every eventuality. Using a silencer to mask the sound and deliver two shots to the head is standard. Loading a single bullet is the action of an amateur. The gunman panicked at the sight of blood. Probably, they never meant to kill Gerry Hogan, just frighten him. The gunman hadn't prepared for something like that to happen, so they had to think fast. They took the gloves from the body to wipe their fingerprints from the weapon. Then they wrapped the small handgun in the gloves and escaped."

"On foot?" asked Neil.

"There are three bus services and four stops on the Common, Neil," said Blessing. "Our killer could have arrived at the Hogan house at six-thirty. I've checked the times. When he ran away, sometime between six-thirty and six-forty-five, he wouldn't have wanted to jump on a bus straight away. The driver, or a passenger, might remember him. He got rid of the gun in the drain and then ditched the gloves in a bin he passed."

"Can you see any flaws in that scenario?" asked Gus.

"We still don't have a motive, guv," said Lydia. "It sounds like a plausible sequence of events, but why was the stranger there in the first place?"

"The only source for that information is at the Hub," said Luke.

"That was a long shot, at best," said Alex.

"Where do we go if Divya doesn't find a suitable candidate?" asked Luke.

"The answers to these questions and more in tomorrow's episode," said Neil.

"I admire your confidence, Neil," said Gus. "You heard Blessing's theory of how things went based on the facts we have. Is there an alternative scenario?"

"Not one I can justify with irrefutable facts, guv," said Neil.

"Back to the drawing board," said Lydia.

"How are you getting on with your file updates, Blessing?"

"Over halfway, guv. Belinda had plenty to say."

"I don't think we can give you guys anything to bite on until the morning. Why don't you have an extra hour at home? Blessing and I will finish here, and we'll see you in the morning. We'll be hanging around until lunchtime, anyway."

Alex and the others didn't need asking twice. They packed up and left.

Gus and Blessing continued updating their digital files.

"I've finished, guv," said Blessing. "Do you mind if I get off home to Worton?"

"No, you can run along, Blessing," said Gus. "I'll be five more minutes."

"How's your jigsaw going, guv?" she asked as she passed his desk.

"I've completed the outside pieces, Blessing," said Gus. "Tomorrow, I hope your pal Divya will deliver the missing pieces to help fill in the gaps in the middle."

Friday, 17 August 2018

GUS HEADED INTO TOWN, ready for a new day at the office. He and Suzie had enjoyed their planned quiet night at home. They talked and listened to music. Gus considered the case.

After parking the car, Gus took the lift to the first floor. He was the first to arrive.

Gus stood by the whiteboards and went through the details one more time. Where hadn't they looked? What was it about the picture showing Gerry Hogan lying on the driveway that bugged him? Lydia had asked why the stranger was there in the first place. Luke thought the motive for the killing relied entirely on the news they would get from the Hub later.

How was that going to help? The lift returned to the ground floor.

Alex and Lydia emerged from the lift a minute later.

"Does it make any more sense this morning, guv," asked Alex. "Looking at it with a clear head?"

"Picture the crime scene photo with Gerry Hogan wearing white gloves," said Gus. "Does it alter anything that Kirkpatrick and Bennison assumed in the first few hours of their investigation?"

"I can't see why, guv," said Lydia. "If the killer were there to do a job, nothing Hogan said or wore made any difference, did it? The killer might think it odd, but we don't know how long they stood outside, talking or arguing before he shot him."

"You spoke about motive last night," said Gus. "What have we eliminated so far?"

"I did not relate to the business," said Alex.

"We can't find anyone with an axe to grind, guv," said Lydia.

The lift descended to the ground floor once more.

Luke and Blessing were next to arrive. They stopped by the whiteboards to see what Gus and the others were studying. The lift moved as soon as the doors closed. Neil was in the building.

"Not the business, no personal grievances with people we know about," said Gus. "Did the killer shoot Gerry as soon as he stepped outside the front door?"

"No, guv," said Luke. "Rachel removed her headphones before answering the door. She needed time to put them on again and start exercising to her music before the shot, or she would have heard it."

Neil Davis strolled into the office.

"Did I miss anything?" he asked.

"Can you remember the police surgeon's comments in his post-mortem report, Neil?" asked Gus.

"He reminded anyone who read his findings that the primary cause of death at the scene is usually blood loss. If a bullet damages key blood vessels, and there isn't enough time to stop the bleeding, the victim will bleed to death."

"How can you recall that word-for-word, Neil?" asked Blessing.

"Peter Morgan was the police surgeon," said Neil. "Pedantic was his middle name. He added that rider to every report he wrote when there was a head wound that resulted in death."

"What does it mean in our case?" asked Gus. "Anyone?"

"The mortality rate from untreated gunshot wounds to the head is ninety percent and rapid," said Neil. "If Gerry Hogan was dead when Rachel Cummins found him at six forty-five, the gunshot must have occurred soon after Rachel returned to the gym."

"To give him time to bleed out," said Alex. "How does that help us?"

"It tells us that the killer could identify himself," said Lydia.

"And explain why Gerry had to die, guv," said Blessing.

"Why did he have to say a word?" asked Neil. "Why not fire as soon as he saw Gerry?"

"You missed something, Neil," said Gus. "Rachel didn't hear the shot. The man had asked for Gerry Hogan by name. He knew *of* Gerry, even if he didn't know him. Perhaps he gave Gerry the reason for wanting him dead. How long was that gap between Rachel leaving the front door and resuming her exercises, Luke?"

Luke considered the layout of the Trowle Common house. He gauged the distance from the front door, past the kitchen, and to the gym. He imagined Rachel stepping inside, throwing down her towel and putting on the headphones.

"Forty-five seconds at least, guv,"

"The average person speaks at one hundred and twenty words per minute," said Gus. "They had a conversation of at least ninety words. Gerry asked what the guy wanted. Is it possible for the gunman to explain why Gerry had to die in less than a hundred words?"

"If the reason was simple, guv," said Alex.

"And Gerry didn't keep asking questions," said Lydia.

"How does that help, guv?" asked Neil.

"We'll know more when we've got the Hub data, " Gus said. "But it helps build a better picture of our gunman."

"What has it changed then, guv?" asked Alex.

"We started with a tall, white, casually dressed man of

indeterminate age," said Gus. "That was the description DI Kirkpatrick had to work with. After speaking to Rachel Cummins, Luke and I expanded that to a tall, white, scruffy man dressed in casual clothing in his mid-twenties. Someone from a working-class background. Now we have a few more things to add. He might have a criminal record. How would an innocent man know where to get hold of an unlicenced gun? We know he wasn't a seasoned killer because he didn't make basic preparations. He loaded just one bullet into the gun. If he had murder in mind, what would he do if he had a misfire? He removed Gerry's white gloves to help clean the gun."

"How would Gerry Hogan have come into contact with a criminal, guv?" asked Lydia.

"When we discover that, Lydia," said Gus. "We'll be well on the way to solving this mystery."

Everyone moved from the whiteboards to their desks. Gus and Blessing had updated their digital files, so Neil, Luke, Alex, and Lydia had plenty of catching up to do. Gus enjoyed the silence as they concentrated on every word between Gus and Blessing and the victim's sister and eldest son.

Who else could they speak to while waiting for the Hub to pull their finger out?

Gus flicked through the sheets of paper on his desk. What had he done with that contact number Geoff Mercer sent for Vicky Bennison? He found it and decided to give her a call.

Gus waited as the young woman gave the charity's name for which she now worked and introduced herself.

"Good morning, Vicky," said Gus. "My name's Gus Freeman. I believe you know a colleague of mine, DS Neil

Davis. He sends his best wishes. Can you spare us a quarter of an hour this morning?"

"I remember Neil. Does he still have a terrible sense of humour?"

"Some things never change, Vicky," said Gus. "We were both sorry to hear why you left the force."

"Then you'll understand why I'd prefer not to talk to you."

"Neil works with me as part of a cold case review team. Our current case was one you worked on with John Kirkpatrick. Do you remember the Gerry Hogan killing?"

"That must have been five or six years ago. Before I transferred to Thames Valley."

"Six years, yes," said Gus. "Are you still working in Oxford?"

"I'm based in Abingdon. You will not take no for an answer, will you?"

"Fifteen minutes of your time," said Gus. "We've made progress but still have one or two missing pieces. However, something you noticed at the time might help bring Gerry's killer to justice."

Gus sat, waiting, as Vicky considered her next move.

"I take a break at noon. Meet me in the Abbey Gardens. I don't want a police car anywhere near our premises. The people we deal with are as wary of the cops as they are of the villains."

"A sign of the times, Vicky," said Gus. "Don't worry. We'll be discreet. I'll make sure Neil's on his best behaviour."

Gus ended the call.

"Are we off, guv?" asked Neil.

"Vicky Bennison has agreed to give us fifteen minutes in Abingdon. How long will it take to get there?"

"If I'm driving, about ninety minutes, guv," said Neil.

"We'll need to leave by ten," said Gus. "That's not ideal, with the Hub business, but needs must. Alex, you can do the honours. As soon as Divya sends her results through, get the rest of the team working on them. You know what we're looking for."

"Got it, guv," said Alex. "Will you let us know what you get from your meeting before you drive back? It might save us chasing a dead-end if Vicky Bennison provides you with a hot lead."

"Good point, Alex," said Gus. "You never know your luck,"

"We haven't had a lot of good luck on this case, guv," said Lydia.

Gus and Neil left the office a few minutes after ten. Neil drove them out to join the M4 on the other side of Chippenham, and then they left the motorway at Junction 13.

"Ever been here before, guv?" asked Neil as he searched for a car park close to the ruins of the ancient Abbey.

"I can't say I have had the pleasure, Neil," said Gus. "I had a quick look online before we left. The ruins result from the collapse of a later addition. Something that the Victorians termed a folly rather than centuries of decay. Since 2012 the town added 'on Thames' to its name. Perhaps they thought it added a cachet to the place, but it smacks of desperation, don't you think?"

"Abingdon's sixty miles from London, guv," said Neil. "I don't suppose they would have been in a rush to claim the moniker if the Thames was as filthy as it used to be twenty years ago."

"The water is cleaner than in the old days, Neil," said Gus, "but they still get a dead body dragged from the river every week of the year. So there's still work to do."

Neil found a car park, and by ten minutes to twelve, the two detectives had located a quiet corner in the Abbey Gardens.

"You'll recognise Vicky Bennison, I presume?"

"She won't have changed that much in ten years, guv," said Neil. "Despite everything she's been through."

Gus heard a church clock chime in the near distance. He looked across the grass towards the ruined folly. Was this a waste of time?

"Hello, Neil. You must be Gus Freeman. Good morning."

"Blimey, you crept up on us, Vicky," said Neil. "How are you?"

"You two remain seated. I'll stay here under the shade of the tree. Your fifteen minutes have started, Mr Freeman."

Gus knew there was no point in arguing.

"What were your first impressions when you arrived at the house on Trowle Common?"

"It seemed clear enough. Someone had shot Gerry Hogan in the head. His partner and his sons recounted what had happened that evening. A stranger arrived on the doorstep asking to speak to Gerry Hogan. He shot Hogan and left."

"Nothing struck you as odd?" asked Gus.

"Not at all. The following morning, we returned to the house to carry out a door-to-door, looking for witnesses. Nobody saw a thing, but one elderly neighbour remembered hearing something. Unfortunately, he couldn't give us accurate timing. It might have been irrelevant. After that, I drove to Bradford-on-Avon to talk with the victim's sister."

"The news of her brother's death came as a shock," said Gus.

"Nobody had contacted her the previous night," said

Vicky. "I asked John if that was odd. He said the young partner and the sister were bound to be at loggerheads. When the will came to light, that explained everything. No matter where we looked for motive or opportunity, we couldn't tie anyone to the killing. A month later, John and I switched to another case."

"How far did you extend the search?" asked Gus.

"We knew about the victim's early life, but there was nothing there. Why wait thirty years to settle a grievance? I suggested the partner could have had a motive. John asked me to dig into her past."

"Rachel Cummins came from Haslemere, in Surrey," said Gus. "Her mother and father split up eighteen months after she was born."

"That all seemed genuine, Gus. There was only one red flag that I spotted. I showed John, and he dismissed the bloke as being too much of a stretch."

"Go on," said Gus.

"Well, Rachel left home after her mother shacked up with an old boyfriend."

"Lawrence Wallace," said Gus. "He gave Rachel the creeps."

"Wallace didn't have a record, and there were no cautions or instances where a woman had made a complaint against him. I never met the man, so I can't comment. Maybe Rachel was right to be cautious. Wallace's son had a criminal record. Carl Wallace was twenty-eight years old and had committed a range of offences since he was fifteen. John looked at the list. I had to agree that Carl never got accused of a violent offence. John thought that if we widened the net far enough, we'd always find a killer related to someone remotely connected to a name on our list of witnesses."

"The six degrees of separation theory," said Neil.

"Something like that, Neil," said Vicky. "Are you married now?"

"To Melody, yes," said Neil. "We're expecting our first child. What about you?"

"I was living with someone when I got injured. After the physical wounds healed, I was in a dark place, so I can't blame my boyfriend for moving out."

Gus was eager to get the conversation back on track.

"So, you didn't chase up this Carl Wallace character to check he wasn't on Trowle Common that night?" asked Gus.

"John wanted to test other theories closer to home. He thought it was more likely that Gerry Hogan had stolen someone's life savings in a dodgy investment scheme. Unfortunately, that's all the time I can spare, Gus. I have no more to add and need to return to the office."

Vicky stepped out from under the tree and started to walk away.

Gus walked beside her, with Neil following two yards behind them.

"Look, Vicky, we know what happened to you back in 2015," said Gus. "You joined the police to protect and to serve the public. You felt that the public and the police had abandoned you to the mob after you suffered those injuries during the protest march."

"The situation was grave three years ago, Gus. It's a darn sight worse now. There's no chance of any protest being peaceful. Where are they held? Ninety percent of them are in cities, making them impossible to police. There are so many inter-connecting streets for people to join the marchers. The original organisation that arranged the march with the police might attract tens of thousands of peaceful souls on the day. Then all sorts of pond life crawl out from under rocks and get onto their What's App group to publicise their battle plan. They know how we police protests, Gus. Everything we do is choreographed. Extremists, anarchists, racists, you name it, they know every tactic, every weakness, and once they've infiltrated the crowd, they change the nature of the protest. It's not random. They plan every step. Before the hour is out, you've got a riot on your hands."

"You were a great loss to the force, Vicky," said Gus. "The work you're doing here with this independent charity is commendable, but I wish there were a way that we could have found a role for you within the police, away from the front line.."

The trio reached the main street, and Vicky prepared to cross the road.

"This is where we go our separate ways, Gus," she said. "Nice to bump into you again, Neil."

"Don't give up on us just yet, Vicky," said Gus.

Vicky Bennison gave them a brief smile and dashed across the road.

"A troubled young woman, guv," said Neil. "I don't think you'll persuade her to return to the fold."

"Maybe not, Neil," said Gus. "I'll talk to Suzie later. Perhaps she can get through to her."

Chapter Twelve

GUS AND NEIL returned to the car park and headed out of Abingdon towards the motorway.

"Do you think DI Kirkpatrick was too hasty in dismissing this Carl Wallace, guv?"

"I don't like coincidences, Neil," said Gus. "The first thing to do is to find out where he is now. He could be inside. Who knows? We can chat, check his whereabouts in May 2012, and move on if there's nothing there. I'll call Alex. He can start the ball rolling."

"What could be his motive anyway, guv?" said Neil. "If Carl still lived in Surrey, why travel a hundred miles to speak to Gerry Hogan? How would he know Hogan in the first place? Six degrees of separation is about right."

"It made more sense if he'd asked for Rachel," said Gus. "Lawrence Wallace lived with Rachel's mother. Or at least he did when Rachel left home. That situation could have changed by 2012. I should have asked her about that when we spoke the other morning."

"It wasn't something that appeared relevant, guv," said

Neil. "We didn't know this Carl fellow existed until ten minutes ago. Although Rachel thought Lawrence was a creep, he wasn't still with Carl's mother by the sound of it. Carl could have left home already by then. His parents would have thrown him out if he was as much trouble as Vicky reckoned."

"We'll chase it up, Neil, just in case,"

Gus called Alex and passed on the message.

"They've received the information from the Hub, Neil," said Gus. "They're working on it as we speak."

"We should get back to the office by two-fifteen at the latest, guv," said Neil.

"Just under three hours to find a break in this case," said Gus. "I would have liked to have closed it by now. It would have made our night at the Waggon & Horses much better."

Neil made it back to the Old Police Station by two o'clock. Gus hadn't looked at the speedometer while they travelled on the motorway. He was too busy joining the dots. They rode up in the lift to the first floor in silence.

"Right," said Gus. "Tell me the story so far."

"Divya found nothing on Kerry, the girl from South Africa, guv," said Alex. "We can't trace any online presence that fits."

"It wasn't much to go on, was it," said Blessing. "A first name and a massive country."

"Molly, Ruth and Shirley, Mandy and Annette, have all social media accounts," Lydia said. "Molly never married. Ruth's divorced, and Shirley's a widow. Mandy and Annette have been married to the same husbands for over twenty-five years."

"Have you contacted them?" Gus asked.

"Their posts and photos look ordinary, guv," said Luke.

"We can message them and ask whether they remember Gerry Hogan, but what's the point?"

"Why did we want the information in the first place?" asked Gus. "We wanted to rule out the possibility that a partner of one girl had a deep-seated grievance against Gerry Hogan. Deep enough to kill him thirty years after the girls in question had met the bloke. So, phone the girls he slept with and discover whether either is protecting our killer. You won't find the answer among their Facebook page posts."

"Yes, guv," said Luke.

"Did anyone chase up where Carl Wallace is?" asked Gus.

"Malaga, guv," said Blessing. "He's lived there for years. He works as a barman."

"More than six years, or less than six?" asked Gus.

"It's over six years since he's been in court in this country, guv," said Blessing. "I can't confirm the date he left for Spain. I've got an address for him, though, guv."

"Good. Try to find a contact telephone number, Blessing. I can't see the ACC letting us fly to Malaga to interview him. Who's left on that list, Alex?"

"We found Bronwen from Tenby, guv," said Alex.

"One of Nick Barrett's failures," said Gus.

"Exactly, guv. Bronwen Griffiths is married to her third husband, Dewi. They live in Saundersfoot, a few miles along the coast from Tenby. Bronwen has a wide circle of friends, but none of them appears to be the girl Gerry Hogan slept with in Cairns. We've messaged Bronwen to ask whether she can recall the name and hometown of her companion. Unfortunately, we've had no response yet."

"Wasn't there another girl?" asked Gus.

"Julia, from Richmond-on-Thames, guv," said Alex.

"They're all at it, guv," said Neil. "It was plain old Richmond when I was at school."

"Is Julia still merchant banking, Alex?" asked Gus.

"She married a wealthy stockbroker and lives near Newbury racecourse, guv," said Alex.

"I suggest we try the same approach with Julia as with the rest."

"How hard do we push, guv?" asked Luke.

"I suppose you want to tread softly with the women still married. We're looking for a killer, Luke. Rustle a few feathers. Only one of them can have something to hide. You'll get a feeling when you speak to someone trying to side-track you."

Gus picked up the phone. It was almost two-thirty.

"Is Kenneth available, Vera?" he asked.

"He hasn't left early just because it's Friday afternoon, Gus," said Vera. "I'll tell him it's urgent."

"How did you know?" asked Gus.

"It's always urgent when you call him."

"Truelove speaking," said the ACC. "What's the problem, Freeman?"

"We believe we've found a lead in the Hogan case, sir. The man concerned is now living in Spain. DS Bennison flagged him as a possible suspect, but DI Kirkpatrick didn't think it worth pursuing."

"And you do?"

"I do, sir," said Gus, crossing his fingers.

"Run it by DS Mercer," said the ACC. "If he thinks it will result in a positive outcome, do what you need to, Freeman."

Did that include flying to Malaga? Should I check, Gus wondered.

Too late, Kenneth Truelove had gone. Gus called Geoff Mercer.

He explained the sequence of events and asked Geoff whether he could fly out to Malaga with Alex Hardy.

"It sounds sketchy, Gus," said Geoff. "You can't place Wallace at the crime scene. He's not got a record for violence. He was never known to carry a knife, let alone a gun. Why target Hogan? Okay, Carl Wallace's father could know that Rachel Cummins was living with a wealthy man. Maybe, Lawrence Wallace was still in contact with his son. Is it likely that Carl travelled that far with a gun to demand money from Hogan? On what grounds? No, I can't see it. The man outside the house that night could be someone else."

"I'll have to make do with a phone call then, Geoff," said Gus.

"Sorry, Gus," said Geoff. "I'd need more than that to sanction a trip abroad."

Gus knew Geoff was right, but something told him they were onto something.

"I've traced a number for Carl Wallace, guv," said Blessing.

"Good girl," said Gus.

"I've found a Facebook account too, guv," said Lydia.

"Any photos?" asked Gus.

"Dozens," said Lydia.

Gus punched the air.

"Print them off, put them in a folder, and I'll take them to show Rachel Cummins."

Gus left the office at a few minutes past three. He'd called Rachel Cummins, and she'd told him she had a fitness session starting at six-thirty. She sounded pleased to hear from him.

Gus rang the bell on the house at Trowle Common twenty-five minutes later. Rachel answered the door at once.

"Come on in," she said. "How can I help?"

She led him into the kitchen.

"This folder contains random photographs of a man from his early twenties to his early thirties," said Gus. "I want you to take a look and tell me who you think it is."

"Interesting," said Rachel, holding out her hand.

Gus gave her the folder. Rachel placed it on the kitchen table and opened it.

She turned over one casual picture of Carl Wallace after another, then paused, returned to the previous photo, and studied it. Finally, Gus walked around the table and stood beside her. In this photo, Carl Wallace was in his late twenties.

"That's him," she said. "How on earth did you find him? Who is he?"

"How certain are you that this was the man you saw outside this house six years ago?"

"I'm certain," Rachel replied.

"You told us you had never seen him before," said Gus.

"I hadn't," said Rachel. "Why, who is he?"

"His name is Carl Wallace," said Gus. "Now, do you remember him?"

"Wallace? Is he related to Lawrence? I didn't know Lawrence's family. Mum didn't mention them. Lawrence was divorced when he contacted Mum."

"Are Lawrence and your mother still together?" asked Gus.

"I suppose so," said Rachel. "She wasn't happy about my reasons for moving out when I did. We're not close anymore. Why would this man want to kill Gerry?"

"We don't know," said Gus. "He's a small-time criminal.

If he learned somehow from his father that Gerry had money, perhaps he came here demanding cash. We'll find out when we interview him."

"Mum didn't know about Gerry," said Rachel. "I told her in a Christmas card that I'd met someone who was a widower with two sons, but I didn't go into details. Mum wasn't interested. As I said, we're really not close. Does Carl Wallace live near Mum?"

"No, he's abroad at present," said Gus.

"My God," said Rachel. "What will you do now?"

"Fly to Malaga as soon as possible," said Gus.

"It won't bring Gerry back, but at least we might know why he died."

Gus thanked Rachel for her help and drove back to the office.

"What did she say, guv?" asked Lydia when Gus exited the lift.

"First things first, Lydia."

Gus called Geoff Mercer and told him the latest news.

"A positive ID of the potential killer?" said Geoff.

"Yes, Geoff. Can we go and get him now?"

"I'll phone ahead to alert the authorities," said Geoff. "Vera is still here for another thirty minutes. After that, I'll get her to book flights to Malaga for the morning. Will that be OK?"

"If Alex says he can get the day off," said Gus.

Alex Hardy nodded. Lydia Logan Barre sighed.

"Does that mean tonight's bash is off, guv?" asked Neil.

"It means Alex and I will be designated drivers," said Gus. "It's important that we celebrate our past successes, and the rest of you can wish Alex and me luck tomorrow."

"Rachel, guv?" asked Lydia.

"She confirmed that Carl Wallace was the man on the

doorstep. They had never met. Rachel didn't know Lawrence Wallace's family. It's a familiar story; mother and daughter became estranged due to the new relationship. Rachel put distance between her and Lawrence. Mum was upset by the reasons that Rachel gave her. The years rolled by, and Rachel met Gerry. Apart from informing her mother in a throwaway comment in a card that she was in a relationship, she insists that she never mentioned Gerry's name or where they lived."

"Her mother knew that Rachel moved to Bath, guv," said Blessing.

"As Neil said, Rachel advertises her business everywhere," said Lydia. "We trace people through the internet. So if this Carl Wallace thought there was something worth chasing, he could soon locate her whereabouts."

Gus's phone rang. Vera Butler was on the line.

"Five past ten from Bristol," she said. "I knew it was urgent. Pick up the e-tickets from Bob at Reception on your way home. Have a good weekend."

"You too, Vera," said Gus. "Thanks for getting that organised."

Vera rang off. Gus breathed a sigh of relief. That didn't sound like Vera would be arriving at the pub later with Rick Chalmers.

"I need to collect our tickets from London Road, Alex," said Gus. "I'll head home a few minutes early. Can you collect me from the bungalow at seven?"

"No problem, guv," said Alex.

Gus gathered his things and made for the lift.

"See you at nine o'clock in the Waggon & Horses," he said. "The usual place, in the quiet bar at the rear."

As the lift travelled to the ground floor, the others started talking.

"There doesn't appear to be any doubt that we've learned who killed Gerry Hogan," said Luke. "Are we closer to working out why?"

"I still want to know why a small-time criminal travels a hundred miles to demand money with menaces," said Neil. "Okay, Gerry had money, but Wallace could target thousands of homes in the Home Counties. It wasn't something he normally did, either. None of his arrests implies that sooner or later, he'd escalate to murder. What are we missing?"

"I don't think we'll get to the bottom of this until Gus and Alex interview Wallace," said Lydia.

"I might have found something to explain Neil's query," said Blessing. "The last time Carl Wallace was in prison was at HMP Leyhill in Gloucestershire. It's only twenty-odd miles from Trowle Common. Perhaps he didn't return to the Guildford area when he came out. We should check those photos on Facebook for metadata, as we did in the Duncan case. I'll ask Divya tonight. Perhaps we can discover where Wallace was in those photos. He could have been local for a short time, which explains how he knew where Hogan lived."

"Good thinking, Blessing," said Lydia. "We'll tell Gus tonight when we see him. One question he needs to ask Carl Wallace is, did he fly out to Malaga from Bristol Airport shortly after May the sixth, 2012?"

"It's five o'clock," said Neil. "I vote we get off home, have a great night tonight, and pick this up again on Monday morning when Gus and Alex have got our man in custody. Then, we'll add our pieces of the jigsaw to the ones they bring back from Malaga and see whether everything falls into place."

"A good idea, Neil," said Luke. "It's been a long week."

The team shut down their computers and headed for the lift.

As their four cars queued to join the Friday afternoon traffic, Gus Freeman collected his tickets from Reception at London Road.

Gus saw Suzie getting into her car when he returned outside.

"Hi, Gus," she said. "What brings you here at this time of day?"

Gus waved the Ryanair tickets and told her he would miss out on what they had planned for Saturday.

"Never mind," said Suzie. "I'm sure you'll make it up to me. Follow me home and tell me all about it."

As Gus and Suzie drove out of Devizes towards Urchfont, a message appeared in Alex Hardy's inbox. It was from Bronwen Griffiths.

WHEN THEY REACHED THE BUNGALOW, Gus told Suzie what he'd learned and who he'd met.

"Give me Vicky Bennison's number," said Suzie. "I'll give her a ring next week."

Gus fished a scrap of paper he'd brought with him from his shirt pocket.

"I know you'll do your best," he grinned.

"Was Rachel Cummins pleased to see you again?" asked Suzie.

"I got that impression, yes, but my focus was on the case, as always, darling," said Gus.

"Do you want to discuss the case and which way you think it will go?"

"No fear," said Gus, "I won't have a clue until I'm face-to-face with Wallace tomorrow."

"In that case, let's prepare a meal together and then get ready for our night out,"

Suzie drove them to the Waggon & Horses, despite Gus insisting that he should be the designated driver to keep their story straight.

"I'm not drinking, Gus," she said, "but you can drive us home if it makes you feel better."

When Gus walked through the door at nine, Neil and Melody were already in the quiet bar.

"The taxi was early, guv," said Neil.

"Only because Neil asked for one to get us here for half-past eight," said Melody.

Suzie sat with Melody to ask how the pregnancy was going. Neil joined Gus at the bar.

"I won't steal her thunder, guv, but Blessing has news that came to light after you left."

"They've found Lord Lucan?" asked Gus.

"Not yet, guv. Talk of the devil, here's Blessing now. Is that Divya? Nobody said she was a beauty."

"Good evening, guv," said Blessing. "I found a piece of information that might come in useful tomorrow. Carl Wallace served time at Leyhill. Divya will check those photos you showed Rachel this afternoon to see where he was at the time."

"I'll give you the locations on Monday morning, Mr Freeman," said Divya.

"It's Gus when we're socialising, Divya. Thanks. Do we think Wallace was closer to Trowle Common in 2012 than a hundred miles away in Surrey, Blessing?"

"It's entirely possible, guv. You should ask Carl whether he flew from Bristol when he fled after the murder."

Alex and the others piled through the door in the next few minutes. Gus kept buying drinks and chatting with his team members and their partners. They had soon caught up on all the latest gossip. The next hour saw them run through the highlights of the last couple of cases they had completed.

Suzie watched Gus and knew what was going on. The lights were on, but there was nobody home. He was already interrogating Carl Wallace and uncovering those final few pieces of the jigsaw.

When the landlord reminded them that he had to close the bar despite their day jobs, the remaining team members started to make their way home. Blessing and Divya had headed out before eleven. Neil and Melody were last to leave, of course. Luke and Nicky hung around to keep them company on the grass verge outside.

Alex and Lydia set off for Chippenham after Gus reminded Alex to set the alarm.

"Everyone had a good time," said Suzie as Gus drove them back to Urchfont. "Do you want me to tell you what happened?"

"I can multitask," said Gus.

Epilogue

Saturday, 18 August 2018

ALEX ARRIVED on the dot at seven o'clock. Gus was waiting at the front door with his passport and their tickets. They were travelling light. They'd rough it at the airport until the morning if they couldn't get a plane back tonight. How long it took to get things sorted depended on Carl Wallace.

After a typical budget airline flight, they arrived in Malaga.

"Where to now, guv?" asked Alex as they negotiated customs.

"A taxi to Soho Bahia, Alex. The bar where Carl works is called El Gato."

Alex found the taxi rank when they left the airport building.

Fifteen minutes later, they stood on the steps leading up to the bar.

Gus looked behind him. There they were. Geoff hadn't

failed him. A blue-and-white patrol car pulled up by the kerb, and two armed officers got out and joined them.

Carl Wallace stood at the end of the bar with a tray of drinks when he spotted the four men heading inside. Alex wondered whether he was going to make a run for it. He needn't have worried. Carl asked another staff member to take the drinks to a table on the patio.

"I knew someone would come to see me eventually," he said.

The local policia delivered Carl to the nearby station while Gus and Alex followed.

"This could be easy," said Alex. "Carl sounds like he's been rehearsing his confession every day since he flew out."

"We'll see," said Gus.

Their hosts were familiar with various international agencies' processes when apprehending criminals on the Spanish mainland. Gus couldn't fault the interview room setup. The place was warmer than most he'd been in over the years, but everything else looked the same.

The two officers led Carl Wallace into the room and seated him opposite Gus and Alex. One officer left while the other stood to one side. Carl Wallace looked forlorn.

"We'll complete the formalities first, Carl," said Alex. "Then we have a few questions."

Carl nodded. He stared at the table in front of him as Alex went through his spiel.

"When did you arrive here in Malaga?" asked Gus.

"At the end of the first week in May, six years ago. You know that. I flew here the afternoon after it happened."

"Where were you on the sixth of May that year?" asked Alex.

"A place between Trowbridge and Bradford-on-Avon. I went to Gerry Hogan's house."

"How did you learn that Gerry Hogan lived at Trowle Common?" asked Gus.

"I found adverts with Rachel's business address online."

"What led you to believe that Gerry Hogan and Rachel Cummins lived together?"

"My Dad told me Rachel had a sugar daddy. He didn't know him, though. My Dad had lived with Rachel's mother and was bitter about them splitting up a year earlier. There was a history between him and Rachel. Dad didn't explain what it was, but I can guess. He's a lecherous old sod. He knew I needed money fast after coming out of prison. Dad gave me information that he thought would convince Hogan he should cough up. It was one way of getting back at Kate through Rachel."

"Kate?" asked Alex.

"Rachel's Mum, of course. She was always Kate when they were kids, and nobody called her Katherine."

That was interesting, thought Gus. Where's this going?

"So, you went to Trowle Common to blackmail Gerry Hogan?" asked Alex.

"With a Beretta Tomcat to make sure Gerry saw things your way," said Gus.

"What was this information that your Dad passed you?" asked Alex.

"Kate got engaged to Jeff Cummins in the summer of '81," said Carl. "They planned to get married in '82. Kate had relatives in Sydney who couldn't get over for the wedding. Jeff was off on a stag week to Cyprus with his mates, so Kate flew out to see her folks and took internal flights to all the tourist spots before flying home from Darwin ten days after she arrived. If Jeff could have a stag week, she could put the free time to good use. Kate got home on the tenth of April. The wedding went ahead in the third week of April. Rachel was born on the second of January."

"A honeymoon baby," said Alex, "nothing unusual."

"Possibly," said Carl, "but I checked. Kate could have conceived that baby before flying home. Dad and Jeff Cummins got talking one night in a pub eighteen months before Kate threw Dad out. Jeff stole Kate from Dad all those years ago, and Dad was bragging about how he'd got the girl in the end. Jeff laughed in his face."

"Why would he do that?" asked Alex.

"The first thing Kate did when she got home from Australia was to get Jeff into her bed."

"Were they sleeping together before she went on holiday?" asked Gus.

"Yeah, but Jeff said it didn't make sense until he had lived with Kate and Rachel for eighteen months."

"He suspected Rachel wasn't his baby?" asked Gus. "That's why they split. After sleeping with Gerry Hogan, Kate slept with Jeff as soon as possible."

"Give the man a gold star. Dad went home from the pub and asked Kate what had happened in Australia. I mean, how dumb was that? It was the beginning of the end. They argued. Kate said the guy wore a Batman t-shirt on the day they met. She woke up the next morning, and Batman had gone. Kate had no idea who he was or where he lived. They were drunk and didn't use protection. Her first thought was to find the tour guide who had driven the bus. It took all day, but she found the guide in a bar later that evening. The girl could remember the two blokes. She'd brought them into town from the airport earlier in the week. She found Kate their details the next morning. Gerry Hogan and Nick Barrett. Kate flew out of Darwin the next day."

"So, your Dad put two and two together and worked out that Gerry Hogan was Rachel's father," said Alex.

"That had to be worth something, didn't it?" said Carl.

"Why didn't your father act upon the information?" asked Gus.

"He wanted me to screw as much as I could out of Hogan, and we'd split it fifty-fifty."

"So, you bought a gun?" asked Alex.

"In Bristol, yeah, no problem."

"How did you get to Trowle Common?"

"On the bus," said Carl.

"You walked up to the front door, rang the bell, and Rachel answered."

"Eventually," said Carl. "I asked for Gerry Hogan. She called out for him. He stepped outside and asked what I wanted. I told him what I knew. I had the gun in front of me, like this, with my back to the road. So the neighbours didn't see."

Carl held his arms out. An amateur, just as Gus thought.

"What did he do, tell you to take a hike? Then you shot him?" asked Gus.

"No, you've got it all wrong. I went through Dad's story, and when I told him he'd been sleeping with his daughter for the past five years, he went as white as a sheet. I'd never pointed a gun at anyone before. He grabbed my hand and twisted it around until the barrel pointed at his temple. The gun fired. I didn't intend to shoot him; you've got to believe me. He kept squeezing my fingers."

"What did you do next?" asked Gus.

"He wore these stupid white cotton gloves. There was blood and brain matter on both of us. I knew that nobody would believe me if I stuck around and tried to explain it was suicide. My fingers were on the trigger. It was my gun.

So, I took the gloves off, stripped off my shirt, wiped myself down as best I could, and wrapped the gun in the gloves. I ran across the common towards Bradford. It was warm. Nobody took any notice of a guy out running without a shirt. I got rid of the gun down a drain and then stashed the gloves in a train station bin. I jumped on the first train, no matter its direction. Lucky for me, it stopped at Bath Spa. I crashed in Victoria Park and caught a bus to Bristol in the morning. I grabbed my stuff from the squat where I was living and borrowed the cash from a mate to make up the money for a one-way ticket here. Since I arrived here, I've worked in bars and have never been in trouble with the law. I've always had one eye on the door waiting for someone like you to come to arrest me. I didn't kill anyone, honest."

Monday, 20 August 2018

ALEX OPENED his inbox just after nine o'clock to find the return message from Bronwen.

'The girl I met on the plane was always Cat to me because of her t-shirt. Her name was Katie or Katherine, and she came from Surrey, but I can't remember the town's name. Hazel, something.'

"What now, guv?" he asked after he'd shown Gus the message,

"I called Geoff Mercer yesterday. Carl Wallace is flying to the UK under escort. Jeff Cummins agreed to a DNA paternity test. We'll know the results on Thursday or Friday."

"You were inclined to believe Carl Wallace, weren't you guv," said Alex.

"Everything we knew about Gerry Hogan points that way, Alex. He was honest and went out of his way to avoid trouble. When Wallace told him Rachel's mother, Kate, was the girl he slept with that night, everything he had worked so hard to protect was running through his fingers like sand. He could see only one way out."

Friday, 24 August 2018

"THE DNA RESULTS ARE BACK, GUS," said Geoff Mercer. "They confirm that Jeff Cummins is Rachel's biological father."

"Thanks, Geoff," said Gus.

Gus picked up his car keys and headed for the lift. First, he had to inform Rachel Cummins, Sean, and Byron Hogan that Gerry's death was a tragic but genuine mistake.

Next in The Freeman Files series

vinci-books.com/strangebeginnings

In Wiltshire's shadows, a decade-old murder mystery awaits the Crime Review Team.

In Wiltshire, England, the unsolved stabbing of Marion Reeves in 2011 resurfaces, capturing the attention of Gus Freeman and his Crime Review Team. As they delve into Marion's past, they find themselves entangled in a maze of secrets guarded by the wealthy and powerful.

Turn the page for a free preview…

Strange Beginnings: Chapter One

Monday, 20 August 2018

"This must be the first time we've all been here by a quarter to nine," said Neil. "Except the guv, of course. Thanks for a splendid night, Friday, by the way. Melody enjoyed meeting up with everyone."

"Did you all have a relaxing weekend?" asked Luke.

"Hardly," said Alex. "Gus and I didn't get back from Malaga until late on Saturday. Although, I suppose half a weekend is better than none."

"Or it would have been," said Lydia. "I heard from my mother on Saturday lunchtime. My father and his partner flew into Edinburgh later that afternoon. We could not get up there and back before this morning to be with them, especially as Alex slept until noon on Sunday."

"Eleanor decided to allow Chidozie to contact her then?" asked Blessing.

Neil heard the lift descend to the ground floor. Gus Freeman was on his way.

"We need to catch up on your news later," he said. "I don't know about Luke, but I've got no juicy gossip to offer. Instead, Melody and I spent two quiet days with our feet up in the garden."

"I drove to Englishcombe village for Sunday lunch with my parents," sighed Blessing.

"That sounds as if it went well," said Luke. "We want to hear your story later."

Blessing gave a more profound sigh.

Gus entered the office at one minute to nine and was pleasantly surprised to see a full house. He wondered why the conversation had faltered.

"Has Alex filled you in on the finer details of Saturday's events yet?" he asked.

"Not yet, guv," said Alex. "We were just asking one another what we'd been up to since Friday night at the Waggon & Horses."

"Well, I need the loose ends on the Hogan case tied in a neat bow as soon as possible. I want the files ready to deliver to Kenneth Truelove. I'll get my report on Saturday's events into the Freeman Files and then call London Road for a meeting with the big man."

"Have they finally confirmed him as Chief Constable, guv?" asked Neil.

"I called Geoff Mercer yesterday evening, and he updated me on a couple of matters," said Gus. "Yes, the appointment will be effective from the first of next month."

"Is that a permanent appointment, guv?" asked Luke. "You know what I mean. Will he be in post until his scheduled retirement, or will this be until they find another candidate from around the country?"

"Good question, Luke," said Gus. "No doubt, they have

a bright, young thing destined for stardom. Someone who ticks the politically correct boxes."

"They tried that with Sandra Plunkett, guv," said Neil. "Wouldn't it be better to stick with a copper's copper rather than try to appease the minority groups with somebody who isn't up to the task?"

"You'd better not let the top brass at London Road hear you say that, DS Davis," said Gus. "Your career will come to an abrupt halt. I imagine we'll get a new face in eighteen months to two years. Kenneth's wife agreed to postpone her cruises, not cancel them altogether. Eighteen months is a decent time for this team to build on its successful start. My position was always temporary. Once I've knocked you into shape and can let you get on with things without me holding your hand, I'll step aside."

"We'll miss you, guv," said Lydia.

Truth be told, Gus would miss the banter and the thrill of the chase.

Gus sat at his desk reviewing the details of Saturday's journey to the sun-kissed shores of the Mediterranean. He and Alex hadn't seen the sea except as they arrived at the airport. The Playa Malagueta was a mere name on a road sign he'd spotted as they headed towards the police station.

When they left Bristol International, Gus believed they would arrest Gerry Hogan's killer. Carl Wallace was firmly in the frame. It shows you can't judge a book by its cover. Even though violence wasn't his stock-in-trade, there were enough black marks against Carl Wallace's name to suggest they had the right man.

Yet, as soon as Carl had spotted them, their prime suspect was eager to co-operate.

Gus had a hunch that a confession was the last thing on Carl's mind, so it proved. However, when they interviewed him, Carl confirmed many of the elements of his conversation on the doorstep of Hogan's home on Trowle Common.

Carl Wallace had learned from his father, Lawrence, that Rachel Cummins had left her mother's home in Haslemere, Surrey, in 2006. Katherine Cummins had a vague recollection that Rachel moved to the West Country. It hadn't taken Carl long to trace the personal trainer. Wallace was serving a custodial sentence at HMP Leyhill in Gloucestershire, so he had time on his hands.

Carl soon found Rachel advertised extensively both online and in the local press.

Lawrence had told him Katherine reckoned Rachel lived with a wealthy, older man. Neither he nor Kate knew the man's name, but Carl uncovered it. Rachel's business address was the same as that of local business owner Gerald Hogan, a widower with two young sons.

A heated conversation in a bar between Lawrence Wallace and Rachel's father, Jim Cummins, had exposed potential leverage for blackmail. Jim Cummins had got engaged to his girlfriend, Kate, before she flew to Australia to visit relatives. She wanted to see the country before returning for their wedding in April. When she arrived on the second of January, Rachel was a honeymoon baby as far as everyone was concerned, but Jeff Cummins became suspicious.

The marriage ended after eighteen months. During their heated discussion, Lawrence Wallace bragged to Jeff about getting together with Kate, just as he had hoped when they were teenagers. They had been an item in the days before Jeff Cummins arrived in town and stole his girl. In the end, Kate and Lawrence's relationship also foundered. Perhaps she finally realised he was as a big a sleaze as Rachel had always maintained.

Gus did not know what Kate Cummins was doing these days. But Lawrence had held onto the knowledge he'd gained of what her ex-husband had said in their argument. Kate, or Kat as friends often called her, had shared one drunken night of passion with a guy she only knew as Batman because of his t-shirt. Kate discovered Batman's true identity only hours before flying home to the UK from Darwin. The man she slept with was Gerry Hogan.

Lawrence Wallace had convinced himself Gerry had to be Rachel's father. The timing was right. Kate's insistence that she and Jim have sex almost as soon as she'd got home from Heathrow sealed the deal. Jim believed Kate was desperate to cover her tracks.

Lawrence thought Carl was better placed to act on that information. His son had moved to Bristol to live after leaving HMP Leyhill and was familiar with operating on the wrong side of the law.

Carl Wallace had told Gus and Alex that buying the Beretta Tomcat in the city was a piece of cake. He'd taken the train from Temple Meads to Bradford-on-Avon. Hopped on a bus to Trowle Common and walked to Hogan's front door on May the sixth, 2012.

Gus had thought he'd known the sequence of events from there. As Carl Wallace gave them his version, Gus understood why so many people they talked to insisted Gerry Hogan was a decent man. A man who went out of his way to avoid trouble. Someone for whom even the hint of scandal would be avoided at all costs.

As Gerry had stood on his doorstep, listening to Carl Wallace tell him Rachel could be his daughter, his world collapsed around him. The girl with the cat on her t-shirt. It was just so plausible.

Gerry had grabbed the gun Carl pointed at him and

turned it on himself. Suicide was preferable to an accusation of an incestuous relationship.

Everything Carl Wallace told them about what followed the fatal shot made sense of the weapon and the missing white gloves. Carl confirmed he'd dropped the Beretta down a drain and the gloves into a waste bin at the railway station. After a night on a park bench in Bath, Carl had flown to Malaga.

He'd worked hard in local bars for six years and never got into trouble. On Saturday night, Carl had flown back to Bristol under escort, and someone else would get asked this week to prepare a case against him for the CPS. Gus was glad he wasn't involved. Only two people knew whether Carl was lying, and one of them was dead. The CPS would probably cut its losses. No jury would find Carl Wallace guilty of murder, but Carl had taken a gun with him that night, whether or not he intended to use it. Why load one bullet if you didn't plan to fire the weapon? No, there was enough to put Carl Wallace away for five years. Wiltshire's new Chief Constable would have to be satisfied with that.

Alex Hardy interrupted his reverie.

"I've had a return message from Bronwen, guv," he said. "It arrived here not long after we left on Friday afternoon."

"Don't keep us hanging, Alex," said Gus. "Spit it out."

"The girl Bronwen met on the plane was always Cat to her because of her t-shirt. Her name was Katie or Katherine, and she came from Surrey, but Bronwen couldn't remember the town's name. Hazel, something."

"What now, guv?" asked Alex.

"I called Geoff Mercer yesterday, as I said. Under escort, Carl Wallace returned to the UK, and Jeff Cummins has agreed to a DNA paternity test. We'll know the results on Thursday or Friday."

"You were inclined to believe Carl Wallace, weren't you, guv?" said Alex.

"Everything we knew about Gerry Hogan points that way, Alex. He was an honest man who avoided scandal. When Carl Wallace told him Rachel's mother, Kate, was the girl he slept with that night, everything he had worked so hard to protect was running through his fingers like sand. He could see only one way out."

"What a mess," said Lydia.

"I feel sorry for the boys," said Blessing. "They lost their mother in a tragic accident. Now they have to live with the thought their father didn't get murdered in a random attack, but he shot himself. If that wasn't bad enough, both Sean and Byron seemed to like Rachel. How will this affect their relationship now? They could be her half-brothers. Lydia's right. It couldn't be much more of a mess."

"The metadata on those Facebook photographs is academic now, Blessing," said Gus. "I don't suppose Divya has got back to you with news yet, has she?"

"She's only just started work, guv. I'll call her," said Blessing. "If Divya can attach location labels to those images, it will strengthen Carl Wallace's assertion that he stayed in Bristol after leaving Leyhill. The labels will neaten the bow on the files you hand in at London Road."

"That sounds sensible," said Gus. "I'll call Vera Butler in a few minutes to see if our leader will grant me an audience. If I have to leave before you receive the data, perhaps Divya can meet me in the foyer at London Road and hand me the necessary information?"

"I'll tell Divya to keep an eye out for your Ford Focus, guv," said Blessing.

Gus gave Blessing the thumbs-up. However, he still had at least an hour of work before making that trip.

"Those of you whose files are already complete," he said, "can you clear the decks ready for our next case, please?"

Gus heard a groan from somewhere on his left but ignored it. He needed to set up his meeting. He called Vera.

"Good morning, Ms Butler. How are you this fine Monday morning?"

"Not as chipper as you, Mr Freeman. Do you want to know when the Chief Constable is free?"

"If it's not too much trouble," said Gus.

"Noon," said Vera. "He says it will have to be a working lunch."

That made a change, thought Gus. They'd never had lunch before. Before his elevation, a cup of coffee and a sticky bun was the extent of catering to Kenneth Truelove's office. Gus foresaw problems for Geoff Mercer's waistline.

"Are you and Kassie Trotter preparing executive lunches these days?" asked Gus. "Or will it be inedible finger food large corporations have served for decades?"

"Grace Packenham is responsible for the changes, Gus," said Vera.

"I imagine that means vegan food is eaten while attempting a painful-looking position on a yoga mat," said Gus. "I'd prefer a Zoom meeting; if I knew what it was. Lydia understands that stuff. The Packenham woman has got to go. She's disrupting the status quo."

"We'll expect you at noon then?" asked Vera.

"I'll have a completed case file in one hand and the other hand extended to receive our next cold case. If this Packenham regime continues, I might need to join an athletics club to learn the art of baton changing. I could be in and out in seconds."

"There won't be any cold sausages or cheese and

pineapple chunks on cocktail sticks," said Vera. "The food comes from a company that runs a fleet of refrigerated vans to deliver their goods. Their sandwiches, bloomer sandwiches, sub rolls, tortilla wraps, bacon and sausage baps, panini, pasta salads and salads are hand-prepared daily. They use local suppliers to source the best produce whenever possible."

"I hope the public never learns that this outrageous expense is coming out of their wage packets," said Gus. "You mentioned a bacon bap. Please put me down for one. Reduce Geoff Mercer's order from two to one. I'll see you at noon, Vera."

With that, Gus ended the call.

It was time to tie those loose ends together. As Gus stepped through his files, he reflected on the interrupted weekend that had just passed. The trip to Malaga meant there was little time for him and Suzie to do anything on Saturday except eat and sleep.

Suzie told him she had driven to Worton for her final hack around the local tracks and lanes on her favourite horse. Then in the afternoon, she'd called Vicky Bennison for a brief chat. Gus was happy to hear Suzie hadn't let the grass grow under her feet. Vicky wouldn't rush back to work with the people she believed failed her in her hour of need, but Suzie making a move within twenty-four hours of him and Vicky's first meeting showed a commitment to mend fences.

Not that Gus had needed reminding, but soon after Alex dropped him off at the bungalow, Suzie told him she had called the surgery and asked them to arrange her twelve-week scan for the second week in September.

After two plane journeys sandwiching a hot, sticky day, Gus was tired and fell asleep as soon as his head hit the pillow. When he awoke just before seven in the morning, he'd tried to work out when the baby might arrive. His best guess was the second week in February. Gus wondered about the central heating. Would the little mite cope with another Beast from the East like the one that arrived this year?

Gus was still making a mental list of the things he needed to check were in order when Suzie had stirred beside him.

"Are you ready for an early breakfast?" he asked.

"Did you sleep well?" asked Suzie.

"I'm as hale and hearty as any sixty-one-year-old can expect," he'd replied.

"In that case, my vote is for brunch," said Suzie.

Later, after they had got up, showered, dressed, and feasted on waffles, they moved from the kitchen into the lounge. Gus retrieved the file folder from the end of the album rack, and he and Suzie spent an hour with coffee and a notepad, making adjustments to Gus's existing will.

"I need to make *my* will as soon as possible," said Suzie. "Seeing what you had to put together will help me make my way through the jargon. It's not something you consider when you're young. It seems so final."

"In your job, it's a good idea to get something in place," said Gus. "Criminals carry weapons far more often than when I started in uniform. It only takes one idiot with a knife, or worse, to lash out when you're responding to a shout. If there's nothing on paper, it can cause grieving relatives extra headaches they could do without. Anyway, that's enough of the morbid stuff for today. Let's get outside and enjoy the sunshine."

"Not that we're relatives, but I take your point. An afternoon on the allotment it is," said Suzie. "Shall we eat at the Lamb tonight?"

"That sounds like a plan. I have plenty of catching up to do on the allotment. We'll aim to get into the pub by six or half-past and then get back here for an early night."

"Easy, tiger," said Suzie.

"It will be a busy day tomorrow," said Gus. "I need to get a good night's sleep."

"You raise a girl's hopes, then crush them, Gus Freeman."

"I try my best," said Gus.

They left the bungalow just before three o'clock and walked along the lane.

"Do you ever read your horoscope, Gus," asked Suzie as they passed the Lamb.

"Not likely," he'd replied. "Why take any notice of a comment that's so general it's bound to strike a chord with somebody, somewhere. Why do you ask?"

"Our baby will be born under the sign of Aquarius. Bob Marley was an Aquarian."

"Marley? An interesting character. Perhaps we should call the little one Marley? It sounds gender-fluid. That's all the rage, so they tell me."

"Never in a million years," said Suzie. "Anyway, Marley is a girl's name. It comes from Old English and means 'pleasant seaside meadow'. I read it in a magazine at the doctor's when I was there six weeks ago."

"One additional fact every day is the high road to success," said Gus. "Are names another thing I need to add to my mental list?"

"What list?" asked Suzie as they walked through the gates to the allotments.

"Things to do to the bungalow before the baby arrives," said Gus. "I might need a bank loan."

"This is a novel experience for both of us, Gus," said Suzie, grabbing his hand. "We'll sort it out, don't fret."

"Love will find a way," laughed Gus.

"I see you two are in good humour,"

The disembodied voice belonged to Clemency Bentham, who emerged from her potting shed with a trowel and a battered floral sunhat perched on her head.

"Have you taken the day off, Reverend?" said Gus.

"Matins ended over two hours ago, Gus," said Clemency. "Which you would know if you were a regular churchgoer. I celebrated Holy Communion earlier this morning when you were still in bed. So the rest of the day is mine."

Suzie blushed, and Gus spotted it and grinned. Clemency caught the glance that passed between them.

"I tell Bert and Irene they're in danger of becoming Darby and Joan these days," said Clemency. "A couple who are content to spend their lives in quiet devotion. You two aren't far behind."

"I must protest, Reverend," said Gus. "We're not Darby and Joan. We're Ancient and Modern. You must have heard the phrase in your line of work?"

"Here and there, Gus," replied Clemency. "Bert Penman dropped by an hour ago, by the way. You missed him. He took one look at your patch of ground and shook his head. I had better let you and Suzie get stuck into knocking it back into shape."

"You're right, of course," sighed Gus. "I can't go gallivanting around mainland Europe on a Saturday and expect my allotment to tend itself. The next three hours will be a start. We plan on eating in the Lamb later. Will you and Brett be around this evening?"

"We will," said Clemency, "although Bert and Irene have already cried off. There's a series on TV that Irene's keen on watching. Brett plans to record it, so we can watch it when we have time. He's not that bothered about the content, but it gives him something to discuss with his grandfather."

"Provided Bert doesn't fall asleep in the middle of the programme after several pints of cider in the Lamb," said Suzie.

"That's a good point," laughed Clemency. "You know we had to help him home the other night. After that short spell in the hospital, Bert won't admit it, but he was worried for Irene."

The Reverend returned to her potting shed, and Gus retrieved tools from his shed so he and Suzie could start work.

"We'll see you next door later," said Clemency, her gardening done for the day. She scooted towards the gateway, clambered aboard her trusty steed, and guided the old bicycle along the lane.

Gus selected a bunch of carrots to harvest and tried to recall when he last watched a TV series. Something always got in the way of committing an hour or two at the same time every week. As for recording things to watch at a later date, Tess had coped with that. If he missed it, he missed it since Tess died. Just like in the old days when his parents first bought a television.

Anyway, life was too short to binge-watch a considerable number of episodes while the sun was shining.

"A penny for them, Gus," said Suzie.

"I thought of another thing to add to my growing list," said Gus. "It's time to upgrade our television. I might not have much chance to take advantage of any added benefits in the short term, but it could come in handy for you next year."

"If you think I'll have time to sit watching TV, you've got plenty to learn," scoffed Suzie. "What do you want me to do to help?"

"I can harvest many vegetables in August," said Gus. "I've got my carrots in that box by the shed. If you check through my runner beans, beetroots, and courgettes to see what's ready to pick, I'll tackle my second early potatoes before sorting out my onions."

"What about the other rows of potatoes next door?" asked Suzie.

"That's my main crop. After that, I'll look at what's underneath the foliage in the first week in September."

"How do you know when to do everything?" asked Suzie.

"I thought you'd know, being a farmer's daughter," said Gus. "I didn't have a clue when I came to Urchfont with Tess. Bert Penman dispensed his wisdom, and I scribbled it in an unused police notebook at home. If I lost that book, I'd be in trouble. It's in a safe place in the shed."

"My older brothers were the ones who learned the basics of animal husbandry and the like at their father's knee," said Suzie. "Dad always wanted me to stick with the Pony Club and perhaps ride point-to-point the same as he and Mum did when I grew older. He didn't want me driving tractors and combine harvesters. He was happiest when we could ride out together, even if it were to exercise the horses in my teens and early twenties."

"You weren't into the competitive side of things like John and Jackie, then?"

"I had a crack at it for a few years, but once I joined the police, I didn't have the time. So I've kept up my weekly hack around the countryside in all wind and weather. I'll be back in the saddle as soon as possible after next February. That's what's important to me, not trophies and rosettes."

The conversation and gardening continued throughout the afternoon. Time flies when you're having fun; or when you're working alongside someone you love. It came as a surprise to both of them when the church clock struck six o'clock.

"Right," said Gus. "Straight home. Take a shower and ease those aching joints. A change of clothes and we can be back in the Lamb before the church clock has chimed the half-hour."

"You get no argument from me," said Suzie.

While she popped into the pub to book a table, Gus collected the tools and returned them to the shed. He took a long appreciative look at the improvements they'd made and the wooden box full of produce he had to carry back to the bungalow.

"Divya says she'll meet you in the foyer of the main building, guv."

Gus returned to the here and now at the sound of Blessing Umeh's voice.

"Thanks, Blessing," he said. The clock on the wall opposite read eleven twenty-two—time to go.

"Do we have everything ready for the Chief Constable?" Gus asked.

The chorus of voices suggested they had been waiting for him to stop daydreaming for a while.

Gus collected their files together and headed for the lift.

What delights lay in store for him at London Road, he wondered.

Grab your copy...
vinci-books.com/strangebeginnings

About the Author

Ted Tayler is the international bestselling indie author of The Freeman Files and The Phoenix series. Ted lives in the English west country, where his stories are based. He was born in 1945 and has been married to Lynne since 1971. They have three children and four grandchildren.

His thought-provoking mysteries appeal to readers of Sally Rigby, Joy Ellis, Pauline Rowson, and Faith Martin. His action-packed thrillers are a must for fans of Mark Dawson and J. C. Ryan.

Gus Freeman's cold case investigations are carried out with reasoned deduction rather than bursts of frantic action. In each of the twenty-four books, unsolved murder is accompanied by romance, humor, and country life. The core message in the twelve Phoenix novels is that criminals should pay for their crimes. Unfortunately, the current system fails to deliver the correct punishment, so Phoenix helps redress the balance.

Acknowledgments

The love and support of my family; without them, this would have been impossible.

www.ingramcontent.com/pod-product-compliance
Lightning Source LLC
Chambersburg PA
CBHW011427010726
47494CB00011B/2532